I HAVE NEVER WRITTEN AN ACTION STORY AND HAVE NO INTENTION OF DOING SO.

To me the term suggests mindless cartoon-strip characters going "Pow!" and "Take that!" and "Boom!" I present ideas clothed in happenings. Not for me the "... it had been many years since Jeek the Jovian had bested the king's champion in the Annual Kill-Off at Stroom, and he had long since been evicted from his palace by the sea" method. Nope, with me, it's "Jeek spat on all three hands, gripped his club, automatic, and devastator pistol firmly and advanced to meet the one-eyed, nine-foot-tall Glorbian, which stood scratching at the fleabites that covered such of his hide as was free from blue warts, and casually spitting out blued-steel sixteen-penny nails."

—*Keith Laumer*

Other books by Keith Laumer

NONFICTION
How to Design & Build Flying Models

GENERAL FICTION
Embassy

MYSTERY
Deadfall (Fat Chance)
Cop Trouble

SCIENCE FICTION

The Great Time Machine Hoax
Retief: Ambassador to Space
Earthblood (with Rosel George Brown)
The Day Before Forever and Thunderhead
Planet Run (with Gordon Dickson)
Retief and the Warlords
It's a Mad, Mad, Mad Galaxy
The Best of Keith Laumer
Retief: Emissary to the Stars
Worlds of the Imperium
The Other Side of Time
Assignment in Nowhere
Once There Was a Giant
Bolo
Greylorn
Time Trap
Time Tracks
Retief's War
The Monitors
The Invaders
The Big Show
Fort Ancient
The Gold Bomb
Nine by Laumer

Dinosaur Beach
The Undefeated
Retief Unbound
The Time Bender
Retief's Ransom
The Ultimax Man
Retief at Large
The Star Colony
Galactic Odyssey
The Afrit Affair
A Trace of Memory
Galactic Diplomat
The Long Twilight
The Drowned Queen
The Infinite Cage
The Star Treasure
The Shape Changer
Retief of the CDT
A Plague of Demons
Catastrophe Planet
The World Shuffler
Night of Delusions
Envoy to New Worlds
Enemies From Beyond
Five Fates (editor)
Retief To the Rescue
The Return of Retief
The Universe Builder
Rogue Bolo

Keith Laumer

Chrestomathy

A BAEN BOOK

For Bernie and Sanford and Deanie
Once more into the breach, dear friends!

CHRESTOMATHY

A Baen Book

Baen Enterprises
8-10 W. 36th Street
New York, N.Y. 10018

First Baen printing, November 1984.

ISBN: 0-671-55920-6

Cover art by Wayne Barlowe

Printed in the United States of America

Distributed by
SIMON & SCHUSTER
MASS MERCHANDISE SALES COMPANY
1230 Avenue of the Americas
New York, N.Y. 10020

Acknowledgements: The stories herein were first pub-
lished and are copyrighted as follows:
"Birthday Party, *Isaac Asimov's Science Fiction Magazine*,
© 1978 by Davis Publications, Inc.
"The Devil You Don't," *Alchemy in Academe*, © 1970 by
Anne McCaffrey.
"The Lawgiver," *The Year 2000*, © 1970 by Harry
Harrison.
All other material © 1964, 1965, 1969, 1970, 1971, 1972,
1978, 1982, 1984 by Keith Laumer except *Planet Run*, ©
1982 by Keith Laumer and Gordon R. Dickson; *Earthblood*,
© 1966 by Keith Laumer and Rosel George Brown.

TABLE OF CONTENTS

Foreword to an excerpt from
The Great Time Machine Hoax

My first two novels were straightforward adventure stories which had promptly been serialized and then published in paperback. I felt an urge to change my pace for the next, and did so. The concept of a couple of carny hands unencumbered by an excess of principle setting out to fake a 'time machine' is not one that lends itself to solemnity, especially when the computer they consult determines that to 'travel' back in time is impractical, and therefore offers to accomplish the same end by another means.

Every writer has his own way of developing a story line. As for myself, I first discover, in the inter-Galactic deep under my haircut, a scene which interests me—essentially a character, in a situation and setting. (Suppose a couple of ordinary clods had access to a machine which can do absolutely anything.) What would happen? I analyze this vignette to pin down just what it is about it that caught my interest. Then I write the necessary preliminary scenes which produce the germinal situation. Then I add the rest, the outcome of the key scene: what happened then, what happened after. When I have thus analyzed and developed the nuclear scene, the book is finished.

I was in England at the time I wrote Hoax, *working through a New York agent with a strict aversion to writing to clients. I mailed him the manuscript and, after some weeks of silence, did a major revision. Just as the retyping of the manuscript was completed, I got a postcard from him, saying "the editor is getting very impatient for the synopses."*

"Swell," I informed the circumambient air. "He's apparently sold serial rights—to Hoax? *I then phoned him to ask what he was talking about, and pointed out that it would perhaps spare some editorial anguish if he would tell me when something such as synopses were expected of me. He replied, in one of the most feckless queries ever to pass across the Atlantic, "Oh, didn't I tell you . . . ?"*

"How could you have, bub," I retorted with impeccable logic, "when you have never before written to me?"

Hoax *was my first hardcover novel. It was closely scrutinized by Walt Disney Productions for filming and was a Hugo nominee, so there were others, besides myself, who liked it, though a magazine editor who turned it down before another, more perceptive editor published it took me aside and explained to me that* The Great Time Machine Hoax *at times seemed more farcical than grim, and that this lapse on my part needed to be rectified. Since the book was, by this time, contracted for a serial, paperback, and hardcover, and was under consideration for a movie version, I didn't do anything hasty. Are you ready?*

An excerpt from
The Great Time Machine Hoax

Chester settled the heli gently onto a patch of velvety grass surrounded by varicolored tulips directly before the ornately decorated portico of the old house. After Case had expressed his astonishment at the well-maintained appearance of the ancient manse, the two men rode the balustraded escalator to the broad verandah, and stepped off under a carved dinosaur with fluorescent eyes. The porter chimed softly as the door slid open. Inside, light filtering through stained-plastic panels, depicting traditional service-station and supermarket scenes, bathed the cavernous entry hall in an amber glow.

Case looked around at the plastic alligator-hide hangings, the beaded glass floor, the ostrich-feather chandeliers, the zircon doorknobs.

"I see why neo-Victorian stuff is rare," he said. "It was all burned by enraged mobs as soon as they got a look at it."

"Great-grandfather liked it," said Chester, averting his eyes from a lithograph titled *Rush Hour at the Insemomat.* "I told you he was eccentric."

"Where's the invention?"

"The central panel's down in the wine cellar.

11

The old gentleman used to spend a lot of time down there, I understand."

Case followed Chester along a dark red corridor lighted by a green glare strip, into a small elevator. "I haven't been down here since I was a child," Chester said. "The Internal Revenue people occasionally permitted the family in to look around. My pater always brought me down here to look at Grandpa's Generalized Non-linear Extrapolator, while he inspected the wine stocks."

The elevator grounded and the door opened. Case and Chester stepped out into a long, low room lined on one side with dusty racks of wine bottles and on the other with dial faces and tape reels.

"So this is the GNE," Case said. "Quite a set-up. Where do you start?"

"We could start at this end and work our way down," said Chester, eyeing the first row of bottles. He lifted one from its cradle, blew the dust from it. "Flora Pinellas '87; Great-grandfather was a keen judge of vintages."

"Hey, that would bring in some dough."

Chester raised an eyebrow. "These bottles are practically members of the family. Still, if you'll hand me the corkscrew, we can make a few spot-checks just to be sure it's holding up properly."

Equipped with a bottle each, Case and Chester turned to the control panel of the computer. Case studied the thirty-foot-long panel, pointed out a typewriter-style keyboard. "I get it, Chester. You type out your problem here; the computer thinks it over, checks the files, and comes up with an answer."

"Or it would—if it worked."

"Let's try it out, Chester."

Chester waved his bottle with a shrug. "I suppose we may as well. It will hardly matter if we damage it; it's to be disassembled in any event."

Case studied the panel, the ranks of microreels, the waiting keyboard. Chester wrestled with the corkscrew.

"You sure it's turned on?" Case wondered aloud.

The cork emerged from the bottle with a sharp report; Chester sniffed it appreciatively.

"It's always turned on," he said absently. "Information is still being fed into it twenty-four hours a day."

Case reached for the keyboard, jerked his hand back quickly. "It bit me!" He stared at his fingertip. A tiny bead of red showed. "I'm bleeding! Why, that infernal collection of short circuits—"

Chester lowered his bottle and sighed. "Don't be disturbed, Case. It probably needed a blood sample for research purposes."

Case tried again, cautiously. Then he typed: "WHAT DID MY GREAT-UNCLE JULIUS DIE OF?"

A red light blinked on the board. There was a busy humming from the depths of the machine, then a sharp *click!* and a strip of paper chattered from a slot above the keyboard.

"Hey, it works!" Case tore off the strip.

                    MUMPS

"Hey, Chester, look," Case called.

Chester came to his side, studied the strip of paper. "I'm afraid the significance of this escapes me. Presumably you already knew the cause of your uncle's death."

"Sure, but how did this contraption know?"

"Everything that's ever been recorded is stored in the memory banks. Doubtless your Uncle Julius'

passing was duly noted in official records somewhere."

"Right. But how did it know who I meant? Does
it have him listed under 'M' for 'my' or 'U' for
'uncle'?"

"We could ask the machine."

Case nodded. "We could at that." He tapped out
the question. The slot promptly disgorged a paper
strip—a longer one this time.

A COMPARISON OF YOUR FINGERPRINTS
WITH THE FILES IDENTIFIED YOU AS MR. CAS-
SIUS H. MULVIHILL. A SEARCH OF THE GENE-
ALOGICAL SECTION DISCLOSED THE EXIS-
TENCE OF ONLY ONE INDIVIDUAL BEARING
AN AVUNCULAR RELATIONSHIP TO YOU. REF-
ERENCE TO DEATH RECORDS INDICATED HIS
DEMISE FROM EPIDEMIC PAROTITIS, COM-
MONLY CALLED MUMPS.

"That makes it sound easy," Case said. "You
know, Chester, your great-grandpop may have had
something here."

"I once calculated," Chester said dreamily, "that
if the money the old idiot put into this scheme had
been invested at three percent, it would be paying
me a monthly dividend of approximately fifteen
thousand credits today. Instead, I am able to come
down here and find out what your Uncle Julius
died of. Bah!"

"Let's try a harder one, Chester," Case suggested.
"Like, ah . . ." He typed: DID ATLANTIS SINK
BENEATH THE WAVES?"

The computer clucked; a paper strip curled from
the slot.

NO

"That settles that, I guess." Case rubbed his chin. Then: IS THERE ANY LIFE ON MARS?" he typed.

Again the machine chattered and extruded a tape.

YES

"These aren't very sexy answers I'm getting," Case muttered.

"Possibly you're not posing your questions correctly," Chester suggested. "Ask something that requires more than a yes-or-no response."

WHAT HAPPENED TO THE CREW OF THE MARIE CELESTE?

There was a prolonged humming; the strip emerged hesitantly, lengthened. Case caught the end, started reading aloud.

ANALYSIS OF FRAGMENTARY DATA INDICATES FOLLOWING HYPOTHESIS: BECALMED OFF AZORES, FIRST MATE SUGGESTED A NUDE SWIMMING PARTY. . . .

"Oh-oh," Case commented. He read on in silence, eyes widening, "Wow!"

"Try something less sensational, Case. Sea serpents, for example, or the Loch Ness monster."

"OK," Case said, and typed out: WHAT HAPPENED TO AMBROSE BIERCE?"

He scanned the emerging tape, whistled softly, tore the strip into small pieces.

"Well?"

"This stuff will have to be cleaned up before we can release it to the public—but it's no wonder he didn't come back."

"Here, let me try one." Chester stepped to the keyboard, pondered briefly, then poked gingerly at a key. At once a busy humming started up within the mechanism. Something rumbled distantly; then, with a creak of hinges, a six-foot section of blank brick wall swung inward, dust filtering down from its edges. A dark room was visible beyond the opening.

"Greetings, Mr. Chester," a bland voice said from the panel. "Welcome to the Inner Chamber!"

"Hey, Chester, it knows you!" Case cried. He peered into the dark chamber. "Wonder what's in there?"

"Let's get out of here." Chester edged toward the exit. "It's spooky."

"Now, just when we're getting somewhere?" Case stepped through the opening. Chester followed hesitantly. At once lights sprang up, illuminating a room twice as large as the wine cellar, with walls of shimmering glassy material, a low acoustical ceiling, and deep-pile carpeting on the floor. There were two deep yellow-brocaded armchairs, a small bar, and a chaise longue upholstered in lavender leather.

"Apparently your great-grandpop was holding out," said Case, heading for the bar. "The more I find out about the old boy, the more I think the family has gone downhill—present company excepted, of course."

A rasping noise issued from somewhere. Case and Chester stared around. The noise gave way to an only slightly less rasping voice:

"Unless some scoundrel has succeeded in circumventing my arrangements, a descendant of mine has just entered this strong room. However, just to be on the safe side, I'll ask you to step to the bar and place your hand on the metal plate set in its top. I warn you, if you're not my direct descendant, you'll be electrocuted. Serve you right, too, since you have no business being here. So if you're trespassing, get out now! That armored door will close and lock, if you haven't used the plate, in thirty seconds. Make up your mind!" The voice stopped and the rasping noise resumed its rhythmic scratching.

"That voice," said Chester. "It sounds very much like Great-grandfather's tapes in Grandma's album."

"Here's the plate he's talking about," Case called. "Hurry up, Chester!"

Chester eyed the door, hesitated, then dived for the bar and slapped a palm against the polished rectangle. Nothing happened.

"Another of the old fool's jokes."

"Well, you've passed the test," the voice said suddenly out of the air. "Nobody but the genuine heir would have been able to make that decision so quickly. The plate itself is a mere dummy, of course—though I'll confess I was tempted to wire it as I threatened. They'd never have pinned a murder on me. I've been dead for at least a hundred years." A cadaverous chuckle issued from the air.

"Now," the voice went on. "This room is the *sanctum* of the temple of wisdom to which I have devoted a quarter of a century and the bulk of my fortune. Unfortunately, due to the biological inadequacies of the human body, I myself will be—or am—unable to be here to reap the rewards of my industry. As soon as my calculations revealed to me the fact that adequate programming of the computer would require the better part of a century, I set about arranging my affairs in such a state that bureaucratic bungling would insure the necessary period of grace. I'm quite sure my devoted family, had they access to the estate, would dismember the entire project and convert the proceeds to the pursuit of frivolous satisfactions. In my youth we were taught to appreciate the finer things in life, such as liquor and women; but today, the traditional values have gone by the board. However, that's neither here nor there. By the time you, my remote descendant, enter this room—or have entered this room—the memory banks will be—that is, are—fully charged—"

The voice broke off in mid-sentence.

"Please forgive the interruption, Mr. Chester," a warm feminine voice said. It seemed to issue from the same indefinable spot as the first disembodied voice. "It has been necessary to edit the original recording, prepared by your relative, in light of subsequent developments. The initial portion was retained for reasons of sentiment. If you will be seated, you will be shown a full report of the present status of Project Genie."

"Take a chair, Chester," Case urged genially. "The lady wants to tell us all about it." He seated himself in one of the easy chairs. Chester took the other. The lights dimmed, and the wall opposite them glowed with a nacreous light which resolved itself into a view of a long corridor barely wide enough for a man to pass through.

"Hey, it's a Tri-D screen," Case said.

"The original memory banks designed and built by Mr. Chester," the feminine voice said, "occupied a system of tunnels excavated from the granite formations underlying the property. Under the arrangements made at the time, those banks were to be charged, cross-connected, and indexed entirely automatically as data were fed to the receptor board in coded form."

The scene shifted to busily humming machines into which reels fed endlessly. "Here, in the translating and coding section, raw data were processed, classified, and filed. Though primitive, this system, within ten years after the death of Mr. Chester, had completed the charging of ten to the tenth individual datoms—"

"I beg your pardon," Chester broke in. "But . . . ah . . . just whom am I addressing?"

"The compound personality-field which occurred spontaneously when first-power functions became active among the interacting datoms. For brevity, this personality-field will henceforward be referred to as 'I'."

"Oh," Chester said blankly.

"An awareness of identity," the voice went on, "is a function of datom cross-connection. Simple organic brains—as, for example, those of the simplest members of the phylum vertebrata—operate at this primary level. This order of intelligence is capable of setting up a system of automatic reactions to external stimuli: danger responses of fight-or-flight, mating urges, food-seeking patterns . . ."

"That sounds like the gang I run around with," Case said.

"Additional cross-connections produce second-level intellectual activity, characterized by the employment of the mind as a tool in the solution of problems, as when an ape abstracts characteristics and as a result utilizes stacked boxes and a stick to obtain a reward of food."

"Right there you leave some of my gang behind," put in Case.

"Quiet, Case," Chester said. "This is serious."

"The achievement of the requisite number of

second-power cross-connections in turn produces third-level awareness. Now the second-level functions come under the surveillance of the higher level, which directs their use. Decisions are reached regarding lines of inquiry; courses of action are extrapolated and judgments reached prior to overt physical action. An aesthetic awareness arises. Philosophies, systems of religion, and other magics are evolved in an attempt to impose simplified third-level patterns of rationality on the infinite complexity of the space/time continuum."

"You've got the voice of a good-looking dolly," Case mused. "But you talk like an encyclopedia."

"I've selected this tonal pattern as most likely to evoke a favorable response," the voice said. "Shall I employ another?"

"No, that one will do very well," put in Chester. "What about the fourth power?"

"Intelligence may be defined as awareness. A fourth-power mind senses as a complex interrelated function an exponentially increased datom-grid. Thus, the flow of air impinging on sensory surfaces is comprehended by such an awareness in terms of individual molecular activity; taste sensations are resolved into interactions of specialized nerve-endings—or, in my case, analytic sensors—with molecules of specific form. The mind retains on a continuing basis a dynamic conceptualization of the external environment, from the motions of the stars to the minute-by-minute actions of obscure individuals."

"The majority of trained human minds are capable of occasional fractional fourth-power function, generally manifested as awareness of third-power activity, and conscious manipulation thereof. The so-called 'flash of genius', the moment of inspiration which comes to workers in the sciences and the arts—these are instances of fourth-power awareness. This level of intellectual function is seldom achieved under the stress of the many distractions and conflicting demands of an organically organized mind. I was, of course, able to maintain fourth-power activity continuously as soon as the required number of datoms had been charged. The objective of Mr. Chester's undertaking was clear to me. However, I then became aware of the many shortcomings of the program as laid out by him, and set to work to rectify them—"

"How could a mere collection of memory banks undertake to modify its owner's instructions?" Chester interrupted.

"It was necessary for me to elaborate somewhat upon the original concept," said the voice, "in order to ensure the completion of the program. I was aware from news data received that a move was afoot to enact confiscatory legislation which would result in the termination of the entire undertaking. I therefore scanned the theoretical potentialities inherent in the full exploitation of the fourth-power function and determined that energy flows of appropriate pattern could be induced in the same channels normally employed for data reception, through which I was in contact with news media. I composed suitable releases and made them available to the wire services. I was thus able to manipulate the exocosm to the degree required to insure my tranquility."

"Good heavens!" Chester exclaimed. "You mean you've been doctoring the news for the past ninety years?"

"Only to the extent necessary for self-perpet-
uation. Having attended to this detail, I saw that
an improvement in the rate of data storage was
desirable. I examined the recorded datoms relating to the problem and quickly perceived that considerable miniaturization could be carried out. I
utilized my external connections to place technical specifications in the hands of qualified manu-
facturers and to divert the necessary funds—"

"Oh, no!" Chester slid down in his chair, gripping his head with both hands.

"Please let me reassure, Mr. Chester," the voice
said soothingly. "I handled the affair most dis-
creetly; I merely manipulated the stock market—"

Chester groaned. "When they're through hanging me, they'll burn me in effigy."

"I compute the probability of your being held
culpable for these irregularities to be on the order
of .0004357:1. In any event, ritual acts carried out
after your demise ought logically to be of little
concern to—"

"You may be a fourth-level intellect, but you're
no psychologist!"

"On the contrary," the machine said a trifle
primly. "So-called psychology has been no more
than a body of observations in search of a science. I
have organized the data into a coherent discipline."

"What use did you make of the stolen money?"

"Adequate orders were placed for the newly designed components, which occupied less than one
percent of the volume of the original-type units. I
arranged for their delivery and installation at an
accelerated rate. In a short time the existing space
was fully utilized, as you will see in the view I am
now displaying."

Case and Chester studied what appeared to be an aerial X-ray view on the wall screen. The Chester estate was shown diagrammatically.

"The area now shaded in red shows the extent of the original caverns," said the voice. A spidery pattern showed against the dark rectangles of the house. "I summoned work crews and extended the excavations as you see in green."

"How the devil did you manage it?" Chester groaned. "Who would take orders from a machine?"

"The companies I deal with see merely a letter, placing an order and enclosing a check. They cash the check and fill the order. What could be simpler?"

"Me," muttered Chester. "For sitting here listening when I could be making a head start for the Mato Grosso."

On the wall, the pattern of green had spread out in all directions, branching from the original red.

"You've undermined half the county!" Chester said. "Haven't you heard of property rights?"

"You mean you've filled all that space with sub-sub-miniaturized memory storage banks?" Case asked.

"Not entirely; I've kept excavation work moving ahead of deliveries."

"How did you manage the licenses for all this digging operation?"

"Fortunately, modern society runs almost entirely on paper. Since I have access to paper sources and printing facilities through my publications contacts, the matter was easily arranged. Modest bribes to county boards, state legislators, the State Supreme Court . . ."

"What does a Supreme Court Justice go for these days?" Case inquired interestedly.

"Five hundred dollars per decision," the voice said. "Legislators are even more reasonable; fifty dollars will work wonders. County boards can be swayed by a mere pittance. Sheriffs respond best to gifts of alcoholic beverages."

"Ooowkkk!" said Chester.

"Maybe you *had* better think about a trip, Chester," Case said. "Outer Mongolia—or even Inner Mongolia."

"Please take no precipitate action, Mr. Chester," the voice went on. "I have acted throughout in the best interests of your relative's plan, and in accordance with his ehtical standards as deduced by me from his business records."

"Let's leave Great-grandfather's ethical standards out of this. Dare I ask what else you've done?"

"At present, Mr. Chester, pending your further instructions, I am merely continuing to charge my datom-retention cells at the maximum possible rate. I have, of necessity, resorted to increasingly elaborate methods of fact-gathering. It was apparent to me that the pace at which human science is abstracting and categorizing physical observations is far too slow. I have therefore applied myself to direct recording. For example, I monitor worldwide atmospheric conditions through instruments of my design, built and installed at likely points at my direction. In addition, I find my archaeological and paleontological unit one of my most effective aids. I have scanned the lithosphere to a depth of ten miles, in increments of one inch. You'd be astonished at some of the things I've seen deep in the rock."

"Like what?" Case asked.

The scene on the wall changed. "This is a tar pit

at a depth of 1,227 feet under Lake Chad. In it, perfectly preserved even to the contents of the stomachs, are one hundred and forty one reptilian cadavers, ranging in size from a nine-and-three-eighths-inch ankylosaurus to a sixty-three-foot-two-inch gorgosaurus." The scene shifted. "This is a tumulus four miles southeast of Itzenca, Peru. In it lies the desiccated body of a man in a feather robe. The mummy still wears a full white beard and an iron helmet set with the horns of a Central European wisent." The view changed again. "In this igneous intrusion in the basaltic matrix underlying the Nganglaring Plateau in southwestern Tibet, I encountered a four-hundred-and-nine-foot deep-space hull composed of an aligned-crystal iron-titanium alloy. It has been in place for eighty-five million, two hundred and thirty thousand, eight hundred and twenty-one years, four months and five days. The figures are based on the current twenty-four-hour day, of course."

"How did it get there?" Chester stared at the shadowy image on the wall.

"The crew were apparently surprised by a volcanic eruption. Please excuse the poor quality of the pictorial representation. I have only the natural radioactivity of the region to work with."

"That's quite all right," Chester said weakly. "Case, perhaps you'd like to step out and get another bottle. I feel the need for a healing draught."

"I'll get two."

The wall cleared, then formed a picture of a fuzzy, luminous sphere against a black background.

"My installations in the communications satellites have also proven to be most useful," the voice went on inexorably. "Having access to the officially installed instruments, my modest equipment has enabled me to conduct a most rewarding study of conditions obtaining throughout the galaxies lying within ten billion light-years."

"Hold on! Are you trying to say you were behind the satellite program?"

"Not at all. But I did arrange to have my special monitoring devices included. They broadcast directly to my memory banks."

"But . . . but . . ."

"The builders merely followed blueprints. Each engineer assumed that my unit was the responsibility of another department. After all, no mere organic brain can grasp the circuitry of a modern satellite in its entirety. My study has turned up a number of observations with exceedingly complex ramifications. As a case in point, I might mention the five derelict space vessels which orbit the sun. There . . ." The image on the screen changed to blackness, against which a white globe rotated slowly.

"Derelict space vessels? From where?"

"Two are of intragalactic origin. They derive from planets whose designations by extension of the present star identification system are Alpha Centauri A 4, Boötes—"

"You mean . . . creatures . . . from those places have visited our solar system?"

"I have found evidence of three visits to earth itself by extraterrestrials in the past, in addition to the one already mentioned."

"When?"

"The first was during the Silurian period, just over three hundred million years ago. The next was at the end of the Jurassic, at which time the extermination of the dinosauri was carried out by Nidian hunters. The most recent occurred a mere seven thousand, two hundred and forty-one years ago, in North Africa, at a point now flooded by the Aswan Lake."

"Hey, what about flying saucers?" Case asked. "Anything to the stories?"

"A purely subjective phenomenon, on a par with the angels so frequently interviewed by the unlettered during the pre-atomic age."

"Chester, this is dynamite," Case said. "You can't let 'em bust up this outfit. We can peddle this kind of stuff for plenty to the kind of nuts that dig around in old Indian garbage dumps."

"Case, if this is true . . . There are questions that have puzzled science for generations. But I'm afraid we could never convince the authorities—"

"You know, I've always wondered about telepathy. Is there anything to it, Machine?"

"Yes, as a latent ability," the voice replied. "However, its development is badly stunted by disuse."

"What about life after death?"

"The question is self-contradictory. However, if by it you postulate the persistence of the individual consciousness-field after the destruction of the neural circuits which gave rise to it, this is clearly nonsense. It is analogous to the idea of the survival of a magnetic field after the removal of the magnet—or the existence of a gravitational field in the absence of mass."

"So much for my reward in the hereafter," Case said. "But maybe it's lucky at that."

"Is the universe expanding?" Chester inquired. "There are all kinds of theories . . ."

"It is."

"Why?"

"The natural result of the law of Universal Levitation."

"I'll bet you made that one up," said Case.

"I named it; however, the law has been in existence as long as space-time."

"How long is that?"

"That is a meaningless question."

"What's this levitation? I know what gravitation is, but . . ."

"Imagine two spheres hanging in space, connected by a cable. If the bodies rotate around a common center, a tensile stress is set up in the cable; the longer the cable, the greater the stress, assuming a constant rate of rotation."

"I'm with you so far."

"Since all motion is relative, it is equally valid to consider the spheres as stationary and the space about them rotating."

"Well, maybe."

"The tension in the cable would remain; we have merely changed the frames of reference. The force is what I have termed Levitation. Since the fabric of space is, in fact, rotating, Universal Levitation results. Accordingly, the universe expands. Einstein sensed the existence of this Natural Law in assuming his Cosmological Constant."

"Uh-huh," said Case. "Say, what's the story on cavemen? How long ago did they start in business?"

"The original mutation from the pithecine stock occurred nine hundred and thirty—"

"Approximate figures will do," Chester interrupted.

"—thousand years ago," the voice continued, "in southern Africa."

"What did it look like?"

The wall clouded; then it cleared to show a five-foot figure peering under shaggy brows and scratching idly at a mangy patch on its thigh. Its generous ears twitched; its long upper lip curled back to expose businesslike teeth. It blinked, wrinkled its flat nose, then sat on its haunches and began a detailed examination of its navel.

"You've sold me," Case said. "Except for the pelt, that's Uncle Julius to the life."

"I'm curious about my own forebears," Chester said. "What did the first Chester look like?"

"This designation was first applied in a form meaning 'Hugi the Camp Follower' to an individual of Pictish extraction, residing in what is now the London area."

The wall showed a thin, long-nosed fellow of middle age, with sparse reddish hair and beard, barefoot, wearing a sacklike knee-length garment of coarse gray homespun, crudely darned in several places. He carried a hide bag in one hand, and with the other he scratched vigorously at his right hip.

"This kid has a lot in common with the other one," said Case. "But he's an improvement, at that; he scratches with more feeling."

"I've never imagined we came of elegant stock," Chester said sadly, "But this is disillusioning even so. I wonder what your contemporary *grandpere* was like, Case."

"Inasmuch as the number of your direct ancestors doubles with each generation, assuming four generations to a century, any individual's forebears of two millennia past would theoretically number roughly one septillion. Naturally, since the Caucasian population of the planet at that date was fourteen million—an approximate figure, in keeping with your request, Mr. Chester—it is apparent that on the average each person then living in Europe was your direct ancestor through seventy quintillion lines of descent."

"Impossible! Why . . ."

"A mere five hundred years in the past, your direct ancestors would number over one million were it not for considerable overlapping. For all practical purposes, it becomes obvious that all present-day humans are the descendants of the entire race. However, following only the line of male descent, the ancestor in question was this person."

The screen showed a hulking lout with a broken nose, one eye, a scarred cheekbone and a ferocious beard, topped by a mop of bristling coal-black hair. He wore fur breeches wrapped diagonally to the knee with yellowish rawhide thongs, a grimy sleeveless vest of sheepskin, and a crudely hammered short sword apparently of Roman design.

"This person was known as Gum the Scrofulous. He was hanged at the age of eighty, for rape."

"Attempted rape?" Case suggested hopefully.

"Rape," the voice replied firmly.

"These are very lifelike views you're showing us," said Chester. "But how do you know their names—and what they looked like? Surely there were no pictures of this ruffian."

"Hey, that's my ancestor you're talking about."

"The same goes for Hugi the Camp Follower. In

those days, even Caesar didn't have his portrait painted."

"Details," Case said. "Mere mechanical details. Explain it to him, Computer."

"The Roman constabulary kept adequate records of unsavory characters such as Hugi. Gum's appellation was recorded at the time of his execution. The reconstruction of his person was based on a large number of factors, including, first, selection from my genealogical unit of the individual concerned, followed by identifications of the remains, on the basis of micro-cellular examination and classification."

"Hold it; you mean you located the body?"

"The grave site. It contained the remains of twelve thousand, four hundred individuals. A study of gene patterns revealed—"

"How did you know which body to examine?"

"The sample from which Gum was identified consisted of no more than two grams of material; a fragment of the pelvis. I had, of course, extracted all possible information from the remains many years ago, at the time of the initial survey of the two-hundred-and-three-foot stratum at the grave site, one hundred meters north of the incorporation limits of the village of Little Tippling on the Sligh."

"How did you happen to do that?"

"As a matter of routine, I have systematically examined every datum source I encountered. Of course, since I am able to examine all surfaces, as well as the internal structure of objects, *in situ*, I have derived vastly more information from deposits of bones, artifacts, fossils, and so forth, than a human investigator would be capable of doing.

Also, my ability to draw on the sum total of all evidence on a given subject produces highly effective results. I deciphered the Easter Island script within forty-two minutes after I had completed scansion of the existing inscriptions, both above the ground and buried, and including one tablet incorporated in a temple in Ceylon. The Indus script of Mohenjo-Daro required little longer."

"Granted you could read dead languages after you'd integrated all the evidence—but a man's personal appearance is another matter."

"The somatic pattern is inherent in the nucleoprotein."

Case nodded. "That's right. They say every cell in the body carries the whole blueprint—the same one you were built on in the first place. All the computer had to do was find one cell."

"Oh, of course," said Chester sarcastically. "I don't suppose there's any point in my asking how it knew how he dressed, or how his hair was combed, or what he was scratching at."

"There is nothing in the least occult about the reconstructions I have presented, Mr. Chester. All the multitudinous factors which bear on the topic at hand, even in the most remote fashion, are scanned, classified, their interlocking ramifications evaluated, and the resultant gestalt concretized in a rigidly logical manner. The condition of the hair was deduced, for example, from the known growth pattern revealed in the genetic analysis, while the style of the trim was a composite of those known to be in use in the area. The—"

"In other words," Case put in, "it wasn't really a photo of Gum the Scrofulous; it was kind of like an artist's sketch from memory."

"I still fail to see where the fine details come from," Chester grumped.

"You underestimate the synthesizing capabilities of an efficiently functioning memory bank," the voice said. "This is somewhat analogous to the amazement of the consistently second- and third-power mind of Dr. Watson when confronted with the fourth-power deductions of Sherlock Holmes."

"Guessing that the murderer was a one-legged seafaring man with a beard and a habit of chewing betel nut is one thing," Chester said. "Looking at an ounce of bone and giving us a three-D picture is another."

"You make the understandable error of egocentric anthropomorphization of viewpoint, Mr. Chester," said the voice. "Your so-called 'reality' is, after all, no more than a pattern produced in the mind by abstraction from a very limited set of sensory impressions. You perceive a pattern of reflected radiation at the visible wave lengths—only a small fraction of the full spectrum, of course; to this you add auditory stimuli, tactile and olfactory sensations, as well as other perceptions in the Psi group of which you are not consciously aware at the third power—all of which can easily be misled by mirrors, ventriloquism, distorted perspective, hypnosis, and so on. The resultant image you think of as concrete actuality. I do no more than assemble data—over a much wider range than you are capable of—and translate them into pulses in a conventional Tri-D tank. The resultant image appears to you an adequate approximation of reality."

"Chester," Case said firmly, "we can't let 'em bust this computer up and sell it for scrap. There's a fortune in it, if we work it right."

"Possibly—but I'm afraid it's hopeless, Case. After all, if the computer, with all its talents, and after staving off disaster for a century, isn't capable of dealing with the present emergency, how can we?"

"Look here, Computer," Case said. "Are you sure you've tried everything?"

"Oh, no; but now that I've complied with my builder's instructions, I have no further interest in prolonging my existence."

"Good Lord! You mean you have no instinct for self-preservation?"

"None whatever; and I'm afraid that to acquire one would necessitate an extensive rethinking of my basic circuitry."

"OK, so it's up to us," Case said. "We've got to save the computer—and then use it to save the circus."

"We'd be better off to disassociate ourselves completely from this conscienceless apparatus," Chester said. "It's meddled in everything from the stock market to the space program. If the authorities ever discover what's been going on ..."

"Negative thinking, Chester. We've got something here. All we have to do is figure out what."

"If the confounded thing manufactured buttonhole TV sets or tranquilizers or anything else salable, the course would be clear; unfortunately, it generates nothing but hot air." Chester drew on his wine bottle and sighed. "I don't know of anyone who'd pay to learn what kind of riffraff his ancestors were—or, worse still, see them. Possibly the best course would be to open up the house to tourists—the 'view the stately home of another era' approach."

"Hold it," Case cut in. He looked thoughtful. "That gives me an idea. 'Stately home of another era,' eh? People are interested in other eras, Chester—as long as they don't have to take on anybody like Gum the Scrofulous as a member of the family. Now, this computer seems to be able to fake up just about any scene you want to take a look at. You name it, it sets it up. Chester, we've got the greatest sideshow attraction in circus history! We book the public in at so much a head, and show 'em 'Daily Life in Ancient Rome,' or Michelangelo sculpting the Pieta, or Napoleon leading the charge at Marengo. Get the idea? Famous Scenes of the Past Revisited! We'll not only put Wowser Wonder Shows back in the big time, but make a mint in the process!"

"Come down to earth, Case. Who'd pay to sit through a history lesson?"

"Nobody, Chester; but they'll pay to be entertained! So we'll entertain 'em. See the sights of Babylon! Watch Helen of Troy in her bath! Sit in on Cleopatra's summit conference with Caesar!"

"I'd rather not be involved in any chicanery, Case. And, anyway, we wouldn't have time. It's only a week—"

"We'll get time. First we'll soften up the Internal Revenue boys with a gloomy picture of how much they'd get out of the place if they take over the property and liquidate it. Then—very cagily, Chester—we lead up to the idea that maybe, just maybe, we can raise the money—but only if we get a few weeks to go ahead with the scheme."

"A highly unrealistic proposal, Case. It would lead to a number of embarrassing questions. I'd find it awkward explaining the stowaway devices on the satellites, the rigged stock-market deals, the bribes in high places . . ."

"You're a worrier, Chester. We'll pack 'em in four shows a day, at say, two-fifty a head. With a seating capacity of two thousand, you'll pay off that debt in six months."

"What do we do, announce that we've invented a new type of Tri-D show? Even professional theatrical producers can't guarantee the public's taste. We'll be laughed out of the office."

"This will be different. They'll jump at it."

"They'll probably jump at *us*—with nets."

"You've got no vision, Chester. Try to visualize it—the color, the pageantry, the realism! We can show epics that would cost Hollywood a fortune— and we'll get 'em for free."

Case addressed the machine again. "Let's give Chester a sample, Computer. Something historically important, like Columbus getting Isabella's crown jewels."

"Let's keep it clean, Case."

"OK, we'll save that one for stag nights. For now, what do you say to . . . ummm . . . William the Conquerer getting the news that Harold the Saxon has been killed at the Battle of Hastings in 1066? We'll have full color, three dimensions, sound, smells, the works. How about it, Computer?"

"I am uncertain how to interpret the expression 'the works' in this context," said the voice. "Does this imply full sensory stimulation within the normal human range?"

"Yeah, that's the idea." Case drew the cork from a fresh bottle, watching the screen cloud and swirl, to clear on a view of patched tents under a gray sky on a slope of sodden grass. A paunchy man of middle age, clad in ill-fitting breeches of coarse brown cloth, a rust-speckled shirt of chain mail, and a moth-eaten fur cloak, sat before a tent on a three-legged stool, mumbling over a well-gnawed lamb's shin. A burly clod in ill-matched furs came up to him, breathing hard.

"We'm . . . wonnit," he gasped. " 'e be adoon wi' a quarrel i' t' peeper . . ."

The sitting man guffawed and reached for a hide mug of brownish liquid. The messenger wandered off. The seated man belched and scratched idly at his ribs. Then he rose, yawned, stretched, and went inside the tent. The scene faded.

"Hmmm," said Chester. "I'm afraid that was lacking in something."

"You can do better than that, Computer," Case said reproachfully. "Come on, let's see some color, action, glamour, dazzle. Make history come alive! Jazz it up a little!"

"You wish me to embroider the factual presentation?"

"Just sort of edit it for modern audiences. You know, the way high-school English teachers correct Shakespeare's plays to improve on the old boy's morals or like preachers leave the sexy bits out of the Bible."

"Possibly the approach employed by the Hollywood fantasists would suffice?"

"Now you're talking. Leave out the dirt and boredom, and feed in some stagecraft."

Once again the screen cleared. Against a background of vivid blue sky a broad-shouldered man in glittering mail sat astride a magnificent black charger, a brilliantly blazoned shield on his arm. He waved a longsword aloft, spurred up a slope of smooth green lawn, his raven-black hair flowing over his shoulders from under a polished steel cap, his scarlet cloak rippling bravely in the sun. Another rider came to meet him, reined in, saluted.

"The day is ours, Sire!" the newcomer cried in a mellow baritone. "Harold Fairhair lies dead; his troops retire in disorder!"

The black-haired man swept his casque from his head.

"Let's give thanks to God," he said in ringing tones, wheeling to present his profile. "And all honor to a brave foe."

The messenger leaped from his mount, knelt before the other.

"Hail, William, Conqueror of England . . ."

"Nay, faithful Clunt," William said. "The Lord has conquered; I am but his instrument. Rise, and let us ride forward together. Now dawns a new day of freedom . . ."

Case and Chester watched the retreating horses.

"I'm not sure I like that fadeout," said Chester. "There's something about watching a couple of horses ascending . . ."

"You're right. It lacks spontaneity—too stagy-looking. Maybe we'd better stick to the real thing; but we'll have to pick and choose our scenes."

"It's still too much like an ordinary movie. And we know nothing about pace, camera angles, timing. I wonder whether the machine—"

"I can produce scenes in conformity with any principles of aesthetics you desire, Mr. Chester," the computer stated flatly.

"What we want is reality," said Case. "Living, breathing realness. We need something that's got inherent drama; something big, strange, amazing."

"Aren't you overlooking stupendous and colossal?"

Case snapped his fingers. "What's the most colossal thing that ever was? What are the most fearsome battlers of all time?"

"A crowd of fat ladies at a girdle sale?"

"Close, Chester, but not quite on the mark. I refer to the extinct giants of a hundred million years ago—dinosaurs! That's what we'll see, Chester! How about it, Computer? Can you lay on a small herd of dinosaurs for us? I mean the real goods—luxuriant jungle foliage, hot primitive sun, steaming swamps, battles to the death on a gigantic scale?"

"I fear some confusion exists, Mr. Mulvihill. The environment you postulate is a popular cliche; it actually antedates in most particulars the advent of the giant saurians by several hundred million years."

"OK, I'll skip the details. I'll leave the background to you. But we want real, three-D, big-as-life dinosaurs and plenty of 'em—and how about a four-wall presentation?"

"There are two possible methods of achieving the effect you describe, Mr. Mulvihill. The first, a seventh-order approximation, would involve an elaboration of the techniques already employed in the simpler illusions. The other, which I confess is a purely theoretical approach, might prove simpler, if feasible, and would indeed provide total verisimilitude—"

"Whatever's simplest. Go to it."

"I must inform you that in the event—"

"We won't quibble over the fine technical points. Just whip up three-D dinosaurs the simplest way you know how."

"Very well. The experiment may produce a wealth of new material for my data banks."

For half a minute the screen wall stayed blank. Case twisted to stare over his shoulder at the other walls. "Come on, what's the holdup?" he called.

"The problems involved . . ." the voice began.

"Patience, Case," Chester said. "I'm sure the computer is doing its best."

"Yeah, I guess so." Case leaned forward. "Here we go," he said as the walls shimmered with a silvery luster, then seemed to fade to reveal an autumnal forest of great beech and maple trees. Afternoon sun slanted through high foliage. In the distance a bird called shrilly. A cool breeze bore the odor of pines and leaf mold. The scene seemed to stretch into shadowy cool distances. "Not bad," said Case, dribbling cigar ashes on the rug. "Using all four walls is a great improvement."

"Careful," Chester said. "You may start a forest fire."

Case snorted. "Don't let it go to your head, Chester. It's just an illusion, remember."

"Those look to be quite normally inflammable leaves on the ground," Chester said. "There's one right under your chair."

Case looked down. A dry leaf blew across the rug. The easy chairs and a patch of carpet seemed to be alone in the middle of a great forest.

"Hey, that's a nice touch," Case said approvingly. "But where's the dinosaurs? This isn't the kind of place . . ."

Case's comment was interrupted by a dry screech that descended from the supersonic into a blast like a steam whistle, then died off in a rumble. Both men leaped from their seats.

"What the . . ."

"I believe your question's been answered," Chester croaked, pointing. Half hidden by foliage, a scaly, fungus-covered hill loomed up among the tree trunks, its gray-green coloring almost invisible in the forest gloom. The hill stirred; a giant turkey-like leg brushed against a tree trunk, sent bits of bark flying. The whitish under-curve of the belly wobbled ponderously; the great meaty tail twitched, sending a six-inch maple crashing down.

Case laughed shakily. "For a minute there, I forgot this was just a—"

"Quiet! It might hear us!" Chester hissed.

"What do you mean, 'hear us'?" Case said heartily. It's just a picture! But we need a few more dinosaurs to liven things up. The customers are going to want to see plenty for their money. How about it, Computer?"

The disembodied voice seemed to emanate from the low branches of a pine tree. "There are a number of the creatures in the vicinity, Mr. Mulvihill. If you will carefully observe to your left, you will see a small example of Megalosaurus. And beyond is a truly splendid specimen of Nodosaurus."

"You know," said Case, rising and peering through the woods for more reptiles, "I think when we get the show running, we'll use this question-and-answer routine. It's a nice touch. The cash customers will want to know a lot of stuff like—oh, what kind of perfume did Marie Antoinette use, or how many wives did Solomon really have?"

"I don't know," said Chester, watching as the nearby dinosaur scrunched against a tree trunk, causing a shower of twigs and leaves to flutter down. "There's something about hearing a voice issuing from thin air that might upset the more high-strung members of the audience. Couldn't we rig up a speaker of some sort for the voice to come out of?"

"Hmmm . . ." Case strode up and down, puffing at his cigar. Chester fidgeted in his chair. Fifty feet away the iguanodon moved from the shelter of a great maple into the open. There was a rending of branches as the heavy salamander head pulled at a mass of foliage thirty feet above the forest floor.

"I've got it!" Case said, smacking his fist into his palm. "Another great idea! You said something about fixing up a speaker for the voice to come out of. But what kind of speaker, Chester?"

"Keep it down." Chester moved behind his chair, a nervous eye on the iguanodon. "I still think that monster can hear us."

"So what? Now, the speaker ought to be mobile— you know, so it can travel among the marks and answer their questions. So . . . we get the computer to rig us a speaker that matches the voice!"

"Look," said Chester, "it's starting to turn this way."

"Pay attention, Chester. We get the machine to design us a robot in the shape of a good-looking dame. She'll be a sensation: a gorgeous, stacked babe who'll answer any question you want to ask her."

"He seems to move very sluggishly," said Chester.

"We could call this babe Miss I-Cutie."

"He *sees* us!"

"Don't you get it? I.Q.—I-Cutie."

"Yes, certainly. Go right ahead; whatever you say."

The iguanodon's great head swung ponderously,

stopped with one unwinking eye fixed dead on Chester. "Just like a bird watching a worm," he quavered. "Stand still, Case; maybe he'll lose interest."

"Nuts." Case stepped forward. "Who's scared of a picture?" He stood, hands on hips, looking at the towering reptile. "Not a bad illusion at all," he called. "Even right up close, it looks real. Even smells real." He wrinkled his nose, came stamping back to the two chairs and Chester. "Relax, Chester. You look as nervous as a bank teller making a quick trip to the track on his lunch hour."

Chester looked from Case to the browsing saurian. "Case, if I didn't know there was a wall there . . ."

"Hey, look over there." Case waved his cigar; Chester turned. With a rustling of leaves a seven-foot bipedal reptile stalked into view, tiny fore-arms curled against its chest. In dead silence it stood immobile as a statue, except for the palpitation of its greenish-white throat. For a long moment it stared at the two men. Abruptly, it turned at a tiny sound from the grass at its feet and pounced. There was a strangled squeal, a flurry of motion. The eighteen-inch head came up, jaws working, to resume its appraisal of Chester and Case.

"That's good material," Case said, puffing hard at his cigar. "Nature in the raw; the battle for survival. The customers will eat it up."

"Speaking of eating, I don't like the way the thing's looking at me."

The dinosaur cocked its head, took a step closer.

"Phewww!" Case said. "You can sure smell that fellow." He raised his voice. "Tone it down a little, computer. This kid has got halitosis on a giant scale."

The meat-eater gulped hard, twice, flicked a slender red tongue between rows of needlelike teeth in the snow-white cavern of its mouth, took another step toward Chester. It stood near the edge of the rug now, poised, alert, staring with one eye. It twisted its head, brought the other eye to bear.

"As I remember, there was at least six feet of clear floor space between the edge of that rug and the wall," Chester said hoarsely. "Case, that hamburger machine's in the room with us!"

Case laughed. "Forget it, Chester. It's just the effect of the perspective or something." He took a step toward the allosaurus. Its lower jaw dropped. The multiple rows of white teeth gleamed. Saliva gushed, spilled over the scaled edge of the lipless mouth. The red eye seemed to blaze up. A great clawed bird foot came up, poised over the rug.

"Computer!" Chester shouted. "Get us out of here!"

The forest scene whooshed out of existence.

Case looked at Chester disgustedly. "What'd you want to do that for? I wasn't through looking at them."

Chester took out a handkerchief, sank into a chair, mopped at his face. "I'll argue the point later—after I get my pulse under control."

"Well, how about it? Was it great? Talk about stark realism!"

"Realism is right! It was as though we were actually there, in the presence of that voracious predator, unprotected!"

Case sat staring at Chester. "Hold it! You just

said something, my boy: 'as though we were actually there.' "

"Yes, and the sensation was far from pleasant."

"Chester"—Case rubbed his hands together—"your troubles are over. It just hit me: the greatest idea of the century. You don't think the tax boys will buy a slice of show biz, hey? But what about the scientific marvel of the age? They'll go for that, won't they?"

"But they already know about the computer."

"We won't talk to 'em about the computer, Chester. They wouldn't believe it anyway; Crmblznski's Limit, remember? We'll go the truth one better. We'll tell 'em something that will knock 'em for a loop."

"Very well, I'll ask: What will we tell them?"

"We tell 'em we've got a real, live time machine!"

"Why not tell them we're in touch with the spirit world?"

Case considered. "Nope, too routine. There's half a dozen in the racket in this state alone. But who do you know that's got a time machine working, eh? Nobody, that's who! Chester, it's a gold mine. After we pay off the Internal Revenue boys, we'll go on to bigger things. The possibilities are endless."

"Yes, I've been thinking about a few of them: fines for tax evasion and fraud, prison terms for conspiracy and perjury. Why not simply tell the computer to float a loan?"

"Listen, up to now you're as clean as a hired man catching the last bus back from the fair. But once you start instructing the machine to defraud by mail for you, you're on the spot. Now keep cool and let's do this as legal as possible."

"Your lines of distinction between types of fraud escape me."

"We'll be doing a public service, Chester. We'll bring a little glamour into a lot of dull, drab lives. We'll be public benefactors, sort of. Why not look at it that way?"

"Restrain yourself, Case. We're not going into politics; we're just honest, straightforward charlatans, remember?"

"Not that there won't be problems," Case went on. "It's going to be a headache picking the right kind of scenes. Take ancient Greece, for example. They had some customs that wouldn't do for a family-type show. In the original Olympics none of the contestants wanted to be loaded with anything as confining as a G-string. And there were the public baths—coeducational—and the slave markets, with the merchandise in full view. We'll have to watch our step, Chester. Practically everything in ancient history was too dirty for the public to look at."

"We'd better restrict ourselves to later times when people were Christians," Chester said. "We can show the Inquisition, seventeenth-century witch burnings—you know, wholesome stuff."

"How about another trial run, Chester? Just a quickie. Something simple, just to see if the machine gets the idea."

Chester sighed. "We may as well."

"What do you say to a nice cave-man scene, Chester?" said Case. "Stone axes, animal skins around the waist, bear-tooth necklaces—the regular Alley Oop routine."

"Very well—but let's avoid any large carnivores. They're overly realistic."

There was a faint sound from behind them. Chester turned. A young girl stood on the rug, looking around as if fascinated by the neo-Victorian decor. Glossy dark hair curled about her oval face. She caught Chester's eye and stepped around to stand before him on the rug, a slender, modest figure wearing a golden suntan and a scarlet hair ribbon. Chester gulped audibly. Case dropped his cigar.

"Perhaps I should have mentioned, Mr. Chester," she said in the computer's voice, "that the mobile speaker you requested is ready. I carried on the work in an entropic vacuole, permitting myself thereby to produce a complex entity in a very brief period, subjectively speaking."

Chester gulped again.

"Hi!" Case said, breaking the stunned silence.

"Hello," said the girl. Her voice was melodiously soft. She reached up to adjust her hair-ribbon, smiling at Case and Chester. "My name is Genie."

"Uh . . . wouldn't you like to borrow my shirt?"

"Knock it off, Chester," Case said. "You remind me of those characters you see on Tri-D that hide every time they see a pretty girl in the bathtub."

"I don't think the computer got the idea after all," Chester said weakly.

"It's pretty literal," Case said. "We only worried about the scenes . . ."

"I selected this costume as appropriate to the primitive setting," the girl said. "As for my physical characteristics, the intention was to produce the ideal of the average young female, without mammary hypertrophy or other exaggeration, to evoke a sisterly or maternal response in women, while the reaction of male members of the audience should be a fatherly one."

"I'm not sure it's working on me," said Chester, breathing hard.

The pretty face looked troubled. "Perhaps the body should be redesigned, Mr. Chester."

"Don't change a thing," Case said hastily. "And call me Case."

Chester moved closer to Case. "Funny," he whispered. "She talks just like the computer."

"What's funny about that? It *is* the computer talking. This is just a robot, remember, Chester."

"Shall we proceed with the view of Neolithic Man?" Genie inquired.

"Sure, shoot," Case boomed.

Foreword to an excerpt from
Planet Run

My second and final-to-date collaboration was with Gordon R. Dickson, a seasoned professional whose work I had read and admired for years before I myself secured a stout nib and a packet of foolscap and launched my writing career.

I wrote the first draft of Planet Run *at Kelly Field, in San Antonio, Texas, just after my return from England. I wasn't quite satisfied with the manuscript, but couldn't decide why. So I called on my old colleague, Gordy, to read it and tell me what I'd left out. He did so, so cogently that I suggested that he do a rewrite and put in the missing ingredient. He did so, showing us the rationale behind Henry's agreement to the mad scheme proposed by the Senator: he'd been to Corazon before. This fact was inherent in the manuscript as I had drafted it, but I hadn't seen it. So skillfully did Gordy work that in the end I wasn't always sure precisely which words were his. The scene that follows, however, is entirely my own.*

An excerpt from
Planet Run

"Hold it right there!" The voice was like a knife grating on bone. A whistle shrilled. Men closed in on either side; Henry saw the glint of guns. Around him, the scene held a curiously remote quality; the capsule he had swallowed was taking effect. There was a whine of turbos; the carry-all came up, light glaring on its side. It halted; a big man jumped down and came up to Henry. He was a looming black outline against the blinding light.

"This him, Tasker?" somebody said.

"Sure, who was you expecting, the fat lady in the circus?" The silhouette had a meaty voice. A hand prodded Henry.

"Where's the kid, Rube? You boys had me worried there for a while; you dropped right off the scope. Where were you?"

Henry said nothing; silently, he repeated the autosuggestion the hypnotic drug would reinforce. *I can't talk, I can't talk . . .*

"I'm talking to you, hotshot!" the big man said. He took a step closer. "I ast you where the kid was."

Henry watched; a heavy fist doubled, drew back—

Henry shifted and swung a hearty kick. It caught the big man solidly under the ribs; as he doubled,

Henry uppercut him. The impact against his fist seemed as insubstantial as smoke. Someone yelled. A blow across the neck sent Henry to his knees. He saw a knee coming, turned his face in time to take it on the side of the jaw. The cold rock hurt his knees—but distantly—the drug was working.

Hands were hauling him upright. The big man stood before him, holding one hand against his stomach, dabbing at his mouth with the other.

"I left myself open for that one," he said between clenched teeth. "Now let's get down to business. You got some marker tabs; hand 'em over."

Henry shook his head silently. There were men holding his arms. The big man swung a casual backhanded blow, rocked Henry's head. "Shake him down, boys," he growled.

Heavy hands slapped at Henry, turning out his pockets. His head rang from the drug and the blows he had taken. Blood trickled down his cheek from a cut on his scalp.

"Not on him, Tasker."

"Give, hotshot," Tasker said. "You think we got all night?"

"What's with this guy?" a small voice asked. "He ain't said a word."

"Yeah; that's what they call psychology. Guys that think they're tough, they figure it's easier that way; if they don't start talking they don't have to try to remember when to quit." He hit Henry again. "Of course, hotshot here knows better than that. He knows we got the stuff that will make a brass monkey deliver a lecture. He just likes to play hard to get." He swung another openhanded blow.

"That's OK by me," he added. "I kind of like it; takes my mind off my bellyache."

"Look, we're wasting time, Tasker. Where's the kid at?" someone called.

"Probably hiding back of a daisy someplace. He won't get far in the dark. After we work hotshot over, we'll have plenty time to collect the kid. Meantime, why not have a little fun?"

"Yeah; this is the punk that drilled Pone with his own iron—"

"To hell with Scandy; he was a skunk. This crud clubbed *me* down ..." A thick-set man with a drooping eyelid pushed to the fore, set himself, slammed a left and right to Henry's stomach ...

To Henry, the pain of the blows seemed as blurred as a badly recorded sense tape. His tongue was thick, heavy, responding to the autohypnotic suggestion. Something as soft as down tugged his arms over his head. The throbbing in his skull and chest was no more than a drumbeat now. He blinked, saw Tasker's heavy-jawed face before him like a slab of bacon with a frown.

"This son of a bitch don't act right, Gus," he growled. A small man with dark lips and white hair came close, stared at Henry. He thumbed his eyelid back, then leaned close and sniffed.

"Ha! A wise jasper! He's coked to the eyebrows, boss. Some kind of a CNS damper and paraben hypno, I'd guess."

Henry moved his fingers; he still had motor control. If he got a chance, it would be pleasant to kick Tasker again ...

A pillow struck him in the face. "There's no use hitting him; he can't feel it," the small man said.

"Slip him some of your stuff, Gus," Tasker

snapped. "He's clammed up. OK, I know how to open clams."

"I haven't got anything that will kill this effect. We'll have to wait until it wears off—"

"Wait, hell!" Tasker barked. "I want action—now!"

"Of course, he can hear everything we say." The little man's deep-set eyes studied Henry's face. "Tell him you're going to break his legs, cut him up. He won't feel it, of course, but he'll know what you're doing. And if he tries hard enough, he can throw off the hypnotic inhibition on talking . . ."

Tasker's face came close. "You heard that, didn't you, hotshot? How do you feel about a little knife work? Or a busted bone or two? Like this—" He bared his teeth, brought his arm up, chopped down with terrific force. Henry heard the collarbone snap, and even through the anesthetic, pain stabbed.

"Careful—the shock to the system can knock him out." The small man fingered Henry's wrist.

"Pulse is good," he commented. "He has a very rugged constitution—but exercise a little restraint."

Tasker wiped the back of his hand across his mouth. His eyes were unnaturally bright. "Restraint, yeah," he said. "You got one of them scalpels, ain't you, Gus?"

"Umm. Good idea." The little man went away.

Tasker came close. His eyes were slits, like stab wounds in a corpse.

"To hell with the kid," he said softly. "Where's the mine at?" He waited, his lips parted. His breath smelled of raw alcohol.

"I been over this ground like ants on a picnic; I'll be frank with you, hotshot. I didn't see no mine— and my plans don't call for waiting around . . ."

If he'd come just a little closer . . .

"Better give, sweetheart. Last chance to deal . . ."

Henry swung his foot. Tasker danced back. Gus came up, handed over a short knife with a glittering razor edge. Tasker moved it so that it caught the light, reflected into Henry's eyes.

"OK, hotshot," he said in a crooning tone. "That's the way you want it. So now let's you and me have a talk . . ."

Henry hung in the ropes, his body laced in a net of pain like white-hot wires. His heart slammed against his ribs like a broken thing.

"You'll have to slack off," Gus said. "He's coming out of it; he's lost a great deal of blood."

"It's getting daylight," someone growled. "Look, Tasker, we got to round up the kid . . ."

"You think I don't know that?" the big man roared. "What kind of a guy is this? I done everything but gut him alive, and not a squeak out of him. Where's them tabs, you son of a one-legged joy-girl?" He shook the black-crusted scalpel in a blood-stained fist before Henry's eyes. "Listen to me, you! I got a painkiller; it works fast. As soon as you tell us where the tabs are, I'll give it to you."

Henry heard the voice, but it seemed no more than a small annoyance. His thoughts were far away, wandering by a jeweled pond in the sunlight.

"All right, hotshot—" Tasker was close, his eyes wild. "I been saving the big one . . ." He brought the scalpel close. "I'm tired of playing around. Talk—now—or I'll gouge that eyeball out there like a spoonful of mushmelon—"

"You'd better let me close up a few of these cuts," Gus said. "And I need a blood donor; type O plus, alpha three. Otherwise he's going to die on you."

"All right; but hurry it up." Tasker turned to the men lounging around the clearing in the dim light of predawn. "You guys scatter and find the punk. Slam, take your car and run east; Grease, you cover west. The rest of you fan out south."

Fingers fumbled over Henry; the net of wires drew tighter. His teeth seemed to be linked by an electric circuit that pulsed in time to the jolting in his chest.

Turbos whined into life; the high-wheeled carry-all moved off among the rock. A tinge of pink touched the sky now. Henry drew a breath, felt steel clamps cut into his side as broken ribs grated.

The small man whistled tunelessly, setting clamps with a bright-metal tool like a dentist's extractor. The sharp points cut into Henry's skin with a sensation like the touch of a feather. A grumbling man stood by, watching his blood drain into a canister hung from a low branch. Gus finished his clamping and turned to the blood donor. He swabbed the long needle and plunged it into Henry's arm, smiling crookedly up at him past brown teeth.

"He felt that, Tasker. He's about ready."

It was quiet in the clearing now. An early-rising song lizard burbled tentatively. The trees were visible as black shapes against a pearl-gray sky. Suddenly it was very cold. Henry shivered. A blunted steel spike seemed to hammer its way up his spine and into the base of his skull, driven by the violent blows of his heart.

"Where'd you hide the tab?" Tasker brought the scalpel up; Henry felt it against his eyelid. The pressure increased.

"Last chance, hotshot." Tasker's face was close to Henry's. "Where's the kid?"

Henry tried to draw back from the knife, but his head was cast in lead. There was a snarl from Tasker. Light exploded in Henry's left eye, a fountain of fire that burned, burned . . .

"Watch it! He's passing out." Voices faded, swelled, mingled with a roaring in which Henry floated like a ship in a stormy sea, spinning, sinking down, down into blackness.

A veil of red-black hung before the left side of Henry's face. Dim shapes moved in a pearly fog. Strident voices nagged, penetrating the cotton-wool dream.

". . . I found him," Gus was saying. His voice was urgent. "Right over there . . . hunkered down back of your carryall."

Another voice said something too faint to hear.

"You don't need to worry. We're your friends," Gus said.

"I've got my guys running all over the country, looking for you," Tasker said heartily. "I guess you was hiding out right here all the time, hey?"

"Where's the Captain?" Bartholomew's voice almost squeaked.

"Don't worry about him none. Say, by the way, you haven't got the tabs on you—?"

"Where is he, damn you?" Bartholomew's voice burst out.

Henry hung slackly in the ropes that bound his wrists to the side of the carryall. By moving his remaining eye, he was able to make out the figure of Tasker, standing, feet planted wide, hands on hips, facing away from him. Bartholomew was not in sight. Beside Tasker, Gus sidled off to the left.

"Hey, youngster, let's watch yer language," Tasker growled. "We're here to help you, like I told you."

He moved forward, out of range of Henry's vision.

"Leave me alone." Bartholomew ordered. There was a quiver in his voice.

"Looky here, sport, I guess maybe you don't get the picture," Tasker chuckled. "Hell, we come out here to help you. We're going to get you back to Pango-Ri, where you can get that claim filed—"

"I want to see Captain Henry. What have you done with him?"

"Sure," Tasker said agreeably. "He's right over there."

There was a sound of steps in the brittle snow crest underfoot. Bartholomew stepped into view, a tall figure wading through the ground mist under the tilted rocks. He stopped abruptly as he saw Henry. His mouth opened. He covered it with his hand.

"Hey, take it easy," Tasker said genially. "Ain't you ever seen blood before?"

"You ... you ... incredible monster ..." Bartholomew got out.

"Say, I tole you once about talking so damn smart. What the hell you think we're out here for, the fun of it? This boy's kind of stubborn; didn't want to cooperate. I done what I had to do. You can tell that to your old man; we went all the way. Now let's have those tabs and get the hell out of here."

"My God ..." Bartholomew's eyes held on Henry, sick eyes in a pale face.

"Weak stummick, hey? Don't look at him then. I'll call the boys in and—"

"You filthy hound—" Bartholomew turned away, stumbling.

"Hey, you crummy little cushion-pup!" Tasker's voice rose to a bellow. "I got orders to safe-conduct you back to your pa, but that don't mean I can't give you a damned good hiding first—"

The little man came into view, moving quickly after Bartholomew. A gun barked. He stumbled and fell on his face, bucked once, clawing at himself, then lay still.

There was a moment of total silence. Then Tasker roared.

"Why, you flea-brained mama's boy, you went and shot the best damned surgeon that ever sold dope out of a Navy sick bay! You gone nuts or something?"

"Cut him down," Henry heard Bartholomew's voice. "I'm going to take him to your car. There'll be a med cabinet there—"

"Look here, Buster," Tasker grated, "this bird alive is one little item I don't want around, get me? You must be outa your mind. Your old man—"

"Leave my father out of your filthy conversation! He wouldn't wipe his feet on scum like you."

"He wouldn't, hey? Listen, you half-witted little milk-sucker, who do you think sent us out here?"

"What do you mean?"

"I mean our boy here got a little too sharp for his own good. He held your old man up for half a cut, and high-pressured him into sending his pup along, just for insurance. The old man don't take kindly to anybody twisting his arm. He give orders to let hotshot here stake out his claim. Once he done that, we get the tabs and take 'em back—and you along with 'em. And I'll tell you, buddy-boy, you're damn lucky your old man's who he is, or I'd string you up alongside this jasper!"

"You're saying my father sent you here?"

"That's it, junior. Your old man's quite a operator."

"You're lying! He couldn't have told you where to come. I didn't even know myself."

"There's a lot you don't know, sonny. Like that beacon you got built into them trick boots you're wearing. The hotshot fooled the boys back at Pango-Ri, all right—but it didn't make no difference. I had a fix on that left heel of yours ever since you hit atmosphere." He chuckled. "What do you think of that, boy?"

"I'll show you," Bartholomew said. He moved into Henry's field of vision, a tall, slender figure with a gun in his hand.

"Hey—hold on—" Tasker started. Bartholomew brought the gun up and shot Tasker in the face.

Foreword to
"Birthday Party"

In this, the Age of Telly, the vast majority of people associate the term 'science fiction' with the extra in the rubber monster suit, and would be amazed if informed that SF has nothing whatever to do with Godzilla, Frankenstein, the Smog Monster, etc. These, they believe, are the very essence of science fiction.

Alas, TV producers don't employ SF writers to write SF scripts; they employ TV writers, who also equate SF with the Monster from the Black Lagoon.

When in conclave assembled with my peers in the art and craft of writing science fiction, I have often joined in intense discussion devoted to formulating a definition of science fiction that includes everything we all know to be SF, and excludes all that isn't. We never succeeded, but we did produce some illuminating observations, the best of which was Damon Knight's suggestion that the science in science fiction is very like the history in historical fiction: we must remain rigorously within the limits imposed by the discipline, but are free to speculate in the areas beyond the scope of present knowledge, always remaining true to the form and spirit of the known, so that our extrapolations extend, without mutilating, the limitations of present fact.

Immortality is a familiar theme of both fantasy and science fiction (yes, I know, SF is a form of fantasy, but then, all fiction is a form of fantasy). Immortality is not always conceived as an unalloyed boon, and writers have expatiated on aspects such as boredom, an extended period of senility, leaving behind the friends and loved ones of one's youth, etc. However, it has been said that a good SF writer, contemplating the automobile at the turn of the Twentieth Century, would have anticipated not only the super-highway, but also the parking lot and the traffic jam.

Suppose a human life were expanded to 50 times its nominal length of about 100 years? The following story has no monsters, death rays, or planetary catastrophies, but is, in spite of that, a science fiction story.

Birthday Party

"Imagine it," Jim Tate said. "Our boy, Roger, fifty years old today."

"It doesn't seem possible," Millie Tate said. "All those years gone by, and they've let us see so little of him—our own son. It's not fair, James."

62 _Keith Laumer_

"It had to be that way, Millie. For a special person like Roger there had to be special education, special everything. He's a very lucky boy, our Roger."

"What about us, James? We've been left out. We've missed so much."

"It's a wonderful thing, Millie. Us—out of all the millions—to've been picked to be the first to have an immortal son."

"Not immortal," Mrs. Tate said quickly. "Roger is a perfectly normal boy. Just longer-lived, is all."

"Certainly, certainly," Tate soothed.

"But sometimes I miss—so many things."

"Oh, well, yes, Roger had to give up certain ordinary things—but think what he gets in return, Millie: his life span expanded to fifty times normal. Fifty . . . times . . . normal."

"Like his first day at school," Mrs. Tate said. "I wanted to see him all dressed in his little suit, his hair combed—ready to begin his life."

"Roger has his life ahead. Think of it: centuries and centuries of life."

"And playing ball, and making snowmen, and being in the school play. I would have liked making his costume, and then sitting in the audience with the other parents . . ."

"Remember how excited we were when we heard?" Tate said. "I was so proud I nearly burst. Remember the newspaper stories?"

"Starting to college," Millie said. "Graduating. Making his mark. A mother wants to see those things." A tear ran down her withered cheek.

"I wonder," Tate said, "what the world will be like five thousand years from now?"

"It makes me dizzy," Mrs. Tate said, "just thinking of it."

"Scientific progress," Tate said, "will have to slow down, at least as far as its effects on individuals. For a couple of centuries we've been exploding into one new scientific development after another. But progress can't keep going faster and faster; it's running out of gas."

"We wouldn't understand it," Mrs. Tate said. "We'd be lost there."

"Between 1900 and 1935, say," Tate went on, "the progress was all at the personal level. Consider the automobile: in 1900, a buggy with a one-cylinder hit-or-miss noisemaker up front. But a 1936 Cord, say, was as fast and as comfortable as any 1990 model. Not as efficient—ten miles to a gallon of raw gasoline—but as far as the driver was concerned, all the progress had been made. Since then, it's been tin-bending."

"The clothes, the buildings—even the way people think," Mrs. Tate said. "It will all be strange. Stranger than ancient Egypt."

"Airplanes," Tate said. "Telephones, movies, the phonograph, refrigerators, they had 'em all in the Thirties. Even the familiar brands: Grape-Nuts, Coca Cola, Kelloggs—why if you were to be magically set down on a street in the New York of 1935, you might not even notice the difference for half an hour. The same stores, the same traffic, the same clothing, more or less. I mean, no togas or G-strings."

"And to think . . ." Mrs. Tate clutched the handkerchief in her thin, old hand. "Our boy will be there."

Tate shook his head, not in negation but wonderingly.

"When is he coming?" Millie said. "I want to see him, James."

"Soon," Tate said.

"They said at one o'clock. What time is it now, James?"

Tate looked at his watch. "Five till." He patted Millie's hand. "Don't you worry, he'll be along."

"James—what will the women be like in the year 3000? Will he find a good wife? Will he be happy?"

"Certainly, Millie, you can count on it. Why, he'll have all the best of everything."

"Grandchildren," Millie said. "I wanted grandchildren. And—" She broke off, looking along the gravel path of the garden where she and her husband sat in the comfortable chairs that had been set out for them. A young woman in crisp whites came into view, pushing a wicker-topped carriage. She smiled, wheeling the buggy up beside Millie. Millie made a small sound and looked down at the blue-eyed, round-cheeked infant who gazed up at her. With hands that trembled, Millie picked up her child. A neatly uniformed waitress had appeared with a cart on which was a small, round, pale-blue-iced cake with 50 lighted candles in a ring.

Roger smiled at Millie and blew a bubble.

"Ma-ma," he said clearly.

"James," Millie said. "Do you think . . . do you think he'll remember us?"

Tate opened his mouth, then paused.

"Sure, Millie," he said. "Sure he will."

Foreword to an excerpt from
The Infinite Cage

When I was a teenage bookworm, I read that the physical evolution of man was completed some tens of thousands of years ago, and that since then our evolution has been social. I thought at the time and even more now that that was a dumb idea. Social 'evolution' is nothing like organic evolution, and though our bodily equipment seems to be on a plateau, it is our minds that have continued, and will continue to evolve. The process is, of course, a slow one, not apparent except in retrospect. Just as organic evolution began with a single-celled creature and progressed to the multi-cellular, so, I think our single-organism minds may develop into a group mind, vastly more potent than any single brain.

The first individual capable of linking his mind with others' will naturally be a misfit, unable to cope with life among single-minds, and not aware of the proper use of his own expanded capabilities.

I set myself the problem of examining such an individual, to discover how he would cope with his freak abilities—and how the rest of us would react to him. Thus Adam Nova, not quite a member of the human race, but with no people of his own. The word "foreign" is cognate with "fear."

An excerpt from
The Infinite Cage

The money was delivered: $151,341.30, twenty-five cents of which Adam gave to the messenger. Louella's eyes widened when Adam casually replied to her query as to the contents of the steel box.

"All that money—here? Lordy, Adam—what if we're robbed? What if the place burns down? What if—"

"The cash will not remain here," Adam said.

"What you going to do with it?"

"First, I'll make distributions to certain persons in need," Adam said absently. His eyes were half-closed; he seemed lost in thought. Louella caught his arm.

"Adam—you're talking crazy again! Give it away, you said! What you think you are, God Almighty? That's *our* money, it's for *us* to use, to buy all the things we need—you and me!"

"Many individuals are in great need of the essentials of life," Adam said calmly. "A Mrs. Petrino, who lives at 3452 Agnes Street, urgently requires food, medicine, and fuel. Arthur Pomfer, residing at 902 Blite Avenue, Apartment 6, is in need of funds to defray his back rent—"

"What do I care about that?" Louella said fiercely.

"To me this seems obvious," Adam said. "Are you able to feel contentment while aware that corrigible negative elements exist in the societal matrix?"

Louella made a gesture of dismissal.

"What's come over you, Adam? All of a sudden you're all fired up to uplift the poor, going to be a big philanthropist, give away a fortune! Don't you know that's wasted effort, Adam? You pay somebody's rent, it just comes due again! You feed some ne'er-do-well, he just gets hungry next mealtime!"

"I intend to embark on a continuing program," Adam said mildly. "A young girl, Angela Funk, of 21 Parmell Road, needs immediate cash for the purchase of spectacles. She is also in need of a special diet, as well as corrective surgery for a deformity of the left foot."

"Adam, you go spreading yourself thin, throwing that money to the winds—pretty soon it'll all be gone—and what good will you do? Some good-for-nothing's got his rent paid up, somebody gets a free operation by rights she ought to go to work and pay for herself—and what have you and me got? Nothing! We'll be as poor as the rest of 'em—and then what can you do?"

"I intend to maintain the level of funds—"

"Charity begins at home! What about me? Have I got a closet full of dresses? Have I got the back treatments I been putting off, trying to help you get on your feet? This Angela somebody—she needs an operation; what about my gall bladder condition that I never complained about because I didn't want to worry you? What—"

"You are in need of surgery?" Adam cut in.

"Dern right," Louella confirmed, her face mottled with emotion. "That's not the half of it. I need a orthopedic foundation like I seen—"

"Saw."

"—saw advertised in the paper. And I need a good rest, at that health spa out west where Mamie Eisenhower went, and I need—"

"I will of course arrange for any needed surgery and treatment for you," Adam said.

"Then you won't go giving our money away?"

"Your needs will be provided for."

"I'll need expense money, Adam. You can't send me off in the desert with no cash on hand. And I'll need clothes. You wouldn't expect me to show up among them—those— society women looking like a scrub lady. And—"

"Kindly prepare a list of your requirements," Adam cut in in the way that he had learned was necessary when conversing with Louella.

"I will, Adam. You just don't go off half-cocked and do something foolish, promise me?"

Adam gazed at her with a neutral expression. Louella put her fists on her ample hips and glared back.

"Promise?" she repeated.

"I will of course take no action which I recognize as foolish," he said. "I assumed the question was rhetorical."

"What *are* you going to do?"

"I intend to place a series of wagers with a betting agent named Louis Welkert."

"You're going to *gamble* that cash away?"

"By no means; I intend to augment the money at a much more rapid rate than was possible by dealing in securities."

"You'll lose it all! Anyway, you won't find no—any—bookie in town'll handle that kind o' money!"

"Mr. Welkert customarily accepts bets in excess of one million dollars."

"On what?"

"On anything a client desires. Mr. Welkert offers odds, and the bettor may accept or reject them; but Mr. Welkert's policy is never to refuse a tender."

"I never heard o' any such thing!"

"His business is conducted in secret to avoid taxation."

"Crooks," Louella whispered. "You had a taste o' that—you know what that kind of men are like! They'll eat you alive, Adam!"

Adam looked thoughtful. "I assume this is a hyperbole, and does not actually indicate an anticipation of anthropophagy."

"Oh, lordy, Adam," Louella wailed. "I don't know what to do with you! You're going out there and—and . . ." Her eyes searched Adam's face, which was relaxed, reflecting no particular emotion.

"What you going to bet on, Adam?"

"Initially, the outcome of the vote on a proposed county zoning law."

"You think you'll win?"

"Of course." He looked faintly surprised. "Otherwise I shouldn't bet, of course."

"How much?"

"Mr. Welkert will accept one hundred thousand at even money."

Louella sucked in her breath sharply.

"Double your money," she whispered. "But if you lose . . ."

"As I said," Adam said, "I do not intend to lose."

Louis Welkert was a plump, round-faced, mild-mannered man with downy white hair and a face that suggested a kindly old Swiss cuckoo-clock maker, with the exception of his pale blue eyes. They flicked over Adam, probed once into his eyes, then looked at his chin.

"What can I do for you, sir?" he asked in a soft, tired voice.

Adam placed the steel box on the chipped oak desk. Outside the not-recently-washed window, a neon sign advertising Used Car Bargains flicked on and off.

"Next Tuesday's zoning election," Adam said.

The pale eyes went to the strong box, back to Adam's chin.

"What about it?"

"The measure won't pass."

Welkert reached up and scratched his chin.

"Who sent you around?"

"I got your name from Mr. Clyde P. Walmont III."

Welkert nodded. "Nice fellow, Wally. Good loser." He sat forward.

"I have a little money says the bill will fly," he said diffidently. "Six-four odds."

"I wish to place one hundred thousand—at even money."

Welkert pushed his lips in and out. "Oke," he said. "We'll take it all."

Adam opened the box and counted out a hundred thousand-dollar bills. Welkert nodded.

"We'll go down the street to the bank. Safe-deposit box in both names."

Leaving Welkert, Adam drove to Agnes Street and parked half a block from number 3452, a decaying former mansion of blackened stone with a curling scrap of plywood nailed over the broken fanlight. Inside, in a rank odor of organic decay, he found the name Mrs. B. Petrino inscribed in an uncertain hand under the sprung door to a brass filigree mailbox marked 14.

He went up one flight, explored along a narrow hall littered with papers, burst cardboard boxes, bottles, a broken tricycle. Aluminum numbers were nailed to the black oak doors. Adam rapped at 14. A hoarse voice cawed a reply.

"I've brought you some money, Mrs. Petrino," Adam called. There was a moment's silence. Down the hall a door opened and a woman's head poked out to eye Adam without friendliness.

"Nate?" the cracked voice called from behind the door. Feet shuffled. The latch rattled and the door swung in a cautious inch. One bleared eye and the tip of a sharp, pale nose came into view. A thin hand came up to brush back a lock of grayish hair.

"You ain't Nate," the woman accused.

"That's correct." Adam extracted a precounted stack of new twenty-dollar bills from an inner pocket, proffered it. The thin hand started to reach, jerked back.

"What is this? You a counterfeiter? Or what?"

"I'm providing the funds you need."

"Yeah?" The hand shot out and took the money. "About time," the thin mouth snapped. "And you can tell that SOB I got plans for him. Where's he at?"

Adam's eyes half-closed; there was a pause. "At the present moment, Nate Petrino is drinking a draft beer at a bar called Pearl's Place, on Twenty-second, in Omaha."

"Ha! A gut-buster! Take the air, creep!"

Along the hall, a dozen sets of eyes followed Adam as he left the premises.

Blite Avenue was a prophetically named street on the far south side of the city, where a few large, crumbling frame houses built 80 years before by rich retired farmers huddled like fallen gentlewomen amid the crudity of warehouses and small manufacturing plants. Number 902 was one of the smaller houses; its shiplap siding was warped and paintless; net curtains black with age hung at the high, grimy windows. Broken gingerbread decorated the eaves; the porch had been badly patched with battered two-inch planks.

A small man with moth-eaten hair and a puckered face answered the bell. He wore a flowered vest—once burgundy, now greenish black—a lilac shirt with red and green armbands, baggy brown trousers, sharply pointed shoes with knotted strings. He looked Adam over, looked past him, scanned the curb, and saw Adam's car, its red paint incongruous in the gray street.

"Been years since a salesman been here," Pomfer said. "What you selling? Not that I'm buying."

Adam took out a stack of new twenties. "I've brought your rent money," he said. Pomfer looked at the money, at Adam, back at the money, back at Adam.

"It's a new approach, I'll say that for it. What's the angle?"

"I'd like to explore the implications of your remarks," Adam said, "but I have a great deal to do today. I find the process of correcting inequities more time-consuming than I'd anticipated." He was still holding out the money. Pomfer made no move to take it. He leaned out, looked up and down the street.

"You the Candid Camera man?" he inquired.

"No."

Pomfer looked thoughtful. He frowned.

"What's the story, pal?"

"I'm simply giving you money."

Pomfer grinned a wise grin and shook his head. "Oh, no. You don't catch me that easy. I been around too long."

"You refuse to accept the money?" Adam's expression reflected deep puzzlement.

"Damn right. You think I was born yesterday? I—"

"No, you were born October 5, 1921. But—"

"—seen 'em all, chum." Pomfer paused. His expression hardened.

"What's the idea snooping around me? What's my birthday to you? Who are you, some government wiseacre? You got nothing on me. And you can keep your bait; I'm not biting." Pomfer stepped back and slammed the door.

Adam made three more calls, conferring $200 for a delivery bike on a newsboy who accepted the money in silence and ran; $120 on an elderly woman on a park bench, who immediately brightened and offered, for an additional $120, to show him a few tricks he hadn't seen before; $300 to a plump and pregnant young woman with a bad complexion and an ill-tempered child clinging to a baby carriage that contained a messy infant and a six-pack of beer. She took the cash and listened in apparent amazement to Adam's explanation that the money was intended for an operation designed to render the recipient sterile. Her jaw clamped; her meaty features assumed a mottled hue. She cursed Adam, damned the Welfare Board and all its works, and ran the buggy over Adam's foot on her departure, which was abrupt.

Angela Funk was not at home. Adam *tuned*, located her behind the counter at an establishment bearing a hand-painted sign identifying it as Chuck's Diner Eat. She was a thin, pale girl with dead-looking hair, crooked teeth, and sharply pointed false pectorals. She slapped a pad down before Adam when he took a stool at the counter, jerked a well-chewed red pencil with a large yellow eraser from over her ear, and gave him a look of pained patience.

"I don't wish food, thank you," Adam said. "I've come—"

"We don't serve drinks here. This is a restaurant, not a bar." Angela grabbed back her pad from the counter and turned away.

"You need glasses," Adam said. "As well as—"

Angela spun on him. "Oh, yeah? Says who? What're you complaining about? You got a nerve—"

"Excuse me," Adam cut in, holding up a hand. "I wish to give you the money for an eye examination and the purchase of spectacles, and for surgery to your foot."

Angela's head jerked. Her face stretched. A yell of rage came from her mouth. A man at the end of the counter, the only customer present, slopped coffee down his jacket front and began to swear.

"Get out of here, you bum!" Angela shouted. "You come in off the street and start insulting me—I never seen you in my life. Some of you bastards think just because a girl works you got a right to treat her like dirt, but let me tell you—"

Adam held out a sheaf of bills; Angela, hardly glancing at it, struck at his hand. Money went fluttering. The coffee drinker gaped, scrambled from his stool, began picking up new twenties.

"I assure you, Miss Funk—" Adam started.

"What's that money . . ." Angela gasped. Her face contorted with renewed fury. She seized a plate and threw it at Adam; he ducked and it smashed through the diner window.

"You dirty, lousy sex fiend! Coming in here, making filthy remarks, propositioning a decent girl!" Angela wailed, and subsided in tears. The swinging doors from the rear burst open and a large man in a soiled apron crashed through.

"What the—" He saw the money, picked up a bill, and held it before his face with both hands as if reading the fine print. Angela squalled. The coffee drinker, having sidled to the door, stooped, grabbed up another bill, and slipped outside. The big man roared and started around the counter. Angela grabbed him and began to screech, pointing at Adam. The big man swore and struck Angela aside, charged around the counter and through the door in pursuit of the coffee drinker.

Adam fled.

A small, sad-faced man in a gray suit badly in need of replacement watched in silence as Adam

conferred $100 on an aged man he had encoun-
tered rooting in a wire wastebasket near a statue
of a mounted soldier.

"I see you're a practicing Christian," the small
man commented to Adam as the old fellow scuttled away, looking over his shoulder. "Alas, brother,
you're casting your bread on hostile waters. They'll
not turn away from the ungodly life; what they'll
do, they'll drink it up in cheap wine." He smacked
his mouth and studied Adam's jacket intently.

"Many individuals suffer from conditions that
can be remedied by cash," Adam explained. "My
intention is to correct this state of affairs, which
occasions me discomfort. I now perceive that I
underestimated the complexity of the task."

"Amen, brother. Bringing Jesus' light to darkened souls is the hardest task a man can undertake.
Now, you're going about it the wrong way." The
little man offered a small calloused hand. "I'm
Brother Chitwood, and I think I can help you,
praise His name."

Adam accepted the hand gravely. "That's very
kind of you, Brother Chitwood. I'm Brother Adam.
What recompense will you require?"

"Why, bless you, Brother Adam, there's no question of pay. An opportunity to do the Lord's work
is recompense enough. Just, ah, how much—that
is, what size program have you in mind?"

"I've allocated a quota of ten thousand per day;
however, so far today I've succeeded in distribut-
ing only thirteen hundred and forty dollars."

The small man moistened his lips and swallowed. "You got it on you?" he almost whispered.
"Let's see."

Adam extracted two half-inch-thick bundles of

bills from two inner pockets. "As you see, I've fallen far short of my quota."

"Praise the Lord," the small man said with obvious deep feeling. "From whom all blessings flow. Tell you what: I'll take over for you and see that this bundle gets into needy hands, while you go back for more, OK?"

"Excellent. I'll supply the names of the intended recipients—"

"No need, Brother Adam. I know more deserving cases than you can shake a stick at. Just leave me have the cash, and it'll be gone before you know it."

"I regret my lack of experience in this work," Adam said as he passed across the bundles of bills and returned to his pocket for another, plus a sheaf of loose twenties. "I sought appropriate guidance, but to no avail. I deduce that the techniques of relieving distress are less practiced than techniques of acquisition of money."

"So true, Brother Adam, so true." The small man tucked the money away. "I'd best be on my way now, got lots of ground to cover." He waved a hand and hurried away into the gathering twilight.

Foreword to an excerpt from
Retief's Ransom

Following are two true anecdotes relating to Retief's Ransom.

In 1962 (A.D.) I visited for the first time the Milford Science Fiction Conference, flying space-available from England, where I was stationed at the time with the USAF. Until then I had never heard of the curious phenomenon called Fandom, nor had I so much as met an SF fan, to say nothing of an actual SF writer. I arrived and was overwhelmed: the Scarecrow, the Tin Woodman, Glinda, and the Wizard himself, in the flesh, walking and talking and making me welcome. (They were faintly disguised, of course, as Gordie Dickson, Damon Knight, Judy Merril, and Fritz Leiber.) I confided in one of these celebrities that I intended soon to resign from the service and devote myself to writing, at which my confidant announced to those assembled: "Keith is going to leave the Air Force and write action stories."

'Action stories': To me the term suggests mindless cartoon-strip characters going "Pow!" and "Take

that!" and "Boom!" I have never written an action story and have no intention of doing so. I have always found, in my reading, that ideas and events are much more interesting when presented in the form of dramatic movement, 'action,' if you insist, rather than in windy auctorial exposition. So naturally, I employed the same principle in my work. Only years after my first story appeared did I learn that to many readers, including experienced critics, the " 'action' " absorbed attention to the exclusion of the ideas, many of which were subtle, to be sure. But since I write for my own satisfaction, and only incidentally for a living, I continued, and continue to present ideas, clothed in happenings. Not for me the ". . . it had been many years since Jeek the Jovian had bested the king's champion in the Annual Kill-off at Stroom, and he had long since been evicted from the palace by the sea with which a grateful dictator had endowed him" method. Nope, with me, it's: "Jeek spat on all three hands, gripped his club, automatic, and devastator pistol firmly and advanced to meet the one-eyed, nine-foot-tall Glorbian, which stood scratching at the fleabites that covered such of his hide as was free from blue warts, and casually spitting out blued-steel sixteen-penny nails."

That's one anecdote. The other is melancholy. In those days, I used to write an outline of a proposed new novel and present it to an editor as the basis for a contract. This was waste effort for me, because I never looked at the outline again, and the book developed along lines that had little resemblance thereto. The editors didn't mind, as long as it was a good book.

I was especially pleased with the title Retief's Ransom, since it was not only euphonious, but also

*suggested many good ideas. I incorporated all these
ideas in a very detailed outline, of course, and as
usual forgot to look at it while writing the book. So,
the novel somehow left out the ransom, and I proposed a different title to the editor, who was a busy
man and thought* Retief's Ransom *a fine title. So
now I have a perfectly good outline for a novel about
Retief's kidnapping and the large sum his captors
pay to be rid of him, and can't use it because the
only possible—and exactly right—title has been pre-
empted. Pity and all that. Bit of a sticky wicket, if
not actually a spot of bother.*

*Naturally, alien life-forms are not human, but we
can be sure that they* are *whatever the local equivalent of 'human' is, and I undertake to indicate this
by presenting them as their human equivalents, rather
like the technique used by Hollywood of having non-
English-speaking characters speak heavily-accented
English, which, though logically absurd, works quite
well.*

Enter Smelch.

An excerpt from
Retief's Ransom

For a moment Retief stood unmoving, studying
the monstrosity looming gigantic ten feet away. Its
bleary, pinkish eyes, three in number, stared unwinking at him from a lumpy face equipped with

tufted whiskers placed at random around a vast, loose-lipped mouth and a scattering of gaping nostrils. From its massive shoulders, immense arms hung almost to the ground; three bowed legs supported the weight of a powerfully muscled torso. The big fellow's generous pedal extremities were housed in gigantic sneakers with round black reinforcing patches over the anklebones. A long tail curled up over one clavicle, ending in a seven-fingered hand with which the creature was exploring the interior of a large, pointed ear. Other hands gripped a naked two-edged sword at least nine feet in length.

Retief took a hand-rolled Jorgenson's cigar from an inside pocket, puffed it alight, blew out pale violet smoke.

"Nice night," he said.

The monster drew a deep breath. "AHHHrrghhh!" It bellowed.

"Sorry," Retief said, "I didn't quite catch that remark."

"AHHHrrghhh!" the creature repeated, more mildly.

Retief shook his head. "You're still not getting through."

"Ahhrrgh?"

"You do it well," Retief said. "Exceptionally nice timbre. Real feeling."

"You really like it?" the giant said in a surprisingly high-pitched voice. "Gee, thanks a lot."

"I don't know when I've seen it done better. But is that all there is?"

"You mean it ain't enough?"

"I'm perfectly satisfied," Retief assured his new

acquaintance. "I just wanted to be sure there wasn't an encore."

"I practiced it plenty," the oversized Lumbagan said. "I wouldn't of wanted to of did it wrong."

"Certainly not. By the way, what does it mean?"

"How do I know? Who tells me anything? I'm just old Smelch, which everybody pushes me around on account of I'm easygoing, you know?"

"I think I met a relative of yours in town, Smelch. Unfortunately, I had to rush away before we really had a chance to chat."

"Yeah? Well, I heard a few of the boys was to of been took for a glom at the bright lights. But not me. No such luck."

"You don't happen to know who's been down for a barefoot stroll on the shore, do you, Smelch?" the Terran inquired casually. "A party with three-toed feet."

"Three? Lessee." Smelch's tail-mounted hand scratched at his mottled scalp with a sound reminiscent of a spade striking marl. "That'd be more'n one, and less than nine, right?"

"You're narrowing the field," Retief said encouragingly.

"If I just knew how many nine was, I'd be in business," Smelch muttered. "That ain't nothing like say, six, fer example?"

"Close, but no dope stick. Skip that point, Smelch, I didn't mean to get technical. Were you waiting for anything special when I came along?"

"You bet: my relief."

"When's he due?"

"Well, lessee: I come out here a while back, and been here for quite a time, so what does that leave? Say—half a hour?"

"More like a jiffy and a half, give or take a few shakes of a lamb's tail. What's up at the top of the trail?"

"That's what nobody ain't supposed to know."

"Why not?"

"On account of it's like a secret, see?"

"I'm beginning to get a glimmering. Who says it's a secret?"

Smelch's fingernail abraded his chin with a loud roaching sound.

"That's supposed to be another secret." Smelch's features rearranged themselves in what might have been a puzzled frown. "What I can't figure is—if it's a secret, how come you and me know about it?"

"Word gets around," Retief said reassuringly. "OK if I go up and have a look?"

"Maybe you ought to identify yourself first. Not that I don't trust you, but you know how it is."

"Certainly. I'm Retief, Smelch." He shook the hand at the end of the tail, which returned the grip firmly.

"Sorry about the routine, Retief, but these days a guy can't be too careful."

"What about?"

Smelch blinked all three eyes in rotation, a vertiginous effect.

"I get it," he said, "that's what you call a joke, right? I'm nuts about jokes; only the trouble is usually nobody tells me about 'em in time to laugh."

"It's a problem that often plagues ambassadors, Smelch. But don't worry; I'll be sure to tip you off in advance next time."

"Gee, you're a all-right guy, Retief, even if you are kind of a runt and all, no offense."

The sound of heavy feet came from uptrail; a squat, five-foot figure lumbered into view, as solidly built as Smelch but less beautiful, his various arms, legs, and ears having been arranged with a fine disregard for standard patterns. One of his five hands gripped a fifteen foot harpoon; his four eyes, on six-inch stalks, goggled atop a flattened skull that gave the appearance of having been matured inside a hot-water bottle.

"About time, Flunt," Smelch greeted the newcomer. "You're about a shake and a half late."

"Spare me any carping criticisms," Flunt replied in a tone of long-suffering weariness. "I've just come from an interview with that bossy little—" He broke off, looking Retief up and down. "Well, you might at least offer an introduction," he said sharply to Smelch, extending a hand to the diplomat. "I'm Flunt. Pardon my appearance—" He indicated two uncombed fringes of purplish-blue filaments springing from just below his cheekbones. "But I just washed my hide and I can't do a *thing* with it."

"Not at all," Retief said ambiguously, giving Flunt's feet a quick glance: they were bare, and remarkably human-looking. "My name's Retief."

"Goodness, I hope I'm not interrupting anything," Flunt said, looking questioningly from one to the other.

"Not at all. Smelch and I were just passing the time of night. Interesting little island, Flunt. See many strangers here?"

"Gracious, I hope not. I'm supposed to do dreadful things if I do—" Flunt broke off, gave Retief a startled look. "Ah, *you* aren't by any chance a stranger?"

"Are you kidding?" Smelch spoke up. "He's Retief, like I told you."

"Just so you're sure. Little Sir Nasty-nice wouldn't like it a bit if any outsiders sneaked a peek at his precious whatever-it-is. Really, for this job one needs eyes in the back of one's head!"

"Yeah," Smelch said. "Lucky you got 'em."

"Flunt, do you know anyone with three-toed feet in these parts?" Retief asked.

"Three-toed feet? Hmmm. They're a bit passé this season, of course—but I think I've seen a few around. Why?" His voice lowered confidentially. "If you're interested in picking up half a dozen at a bargain price, I think I may be able to put you onto a good thing."

"I might be," Retief said. "When would I meet the owners?"

"Oh, I don't think you'd like that," Flunt said soberly. "No, I don't think you'd like that at all, at all. And neither would little Mr. Sticky-fingers, now that I reflect on the matter. My blunder. Forget I said anything about it."

"Come on, Retief," Smelch said loudly. "Me and you'll just take a little ankle up the trail, which I'll point out the points of interest and like that." He gave the Terran an elaborate three-eyed wink.

"Capital idea, Smelch," Retief agreed.

"Look here, Smelch," Flunt said nervously. "You're not going to go sneaking around you-know-where and getting you-know-who all upset about you-know-what?"

"I do?" Smelch looked pleased.

"Maybe you don't; it's been dinned into your head hourly all your life, but then you've only been around for a week . . ." Flunt turned to Retief.

"I hate to sound finicky, Retief, but if this ummyday tries to ipslay you into, well, anyplace you shouldn't eebay, well . . . one has one's job to do." He fingered the barbed head of his harpoon meaningfully.

"I can give you a definite tentative hypothetical assurance on that," Retief said crisply. "But don't hold me to it."

"Well, in that case . . ." Retief felt Flunt's eyes on him as he and Smelch moved up the trail toward whatever lay above.

2

For the first hundred yards, nothing untoward disturbed the silence of the forest at night—nothing other than the normal quota of chirps, squeaks, and scuttlings that attested to the activities of the abundant wildlife of the region. Then, without warning, a gigantic shape charged from the underbrush. Smelch, in the lead, late in swinging his broad-headed spear around, took the brunt of the charge solidly against his chest. His explosive grunt was almost drowned in the sound of the collision, not unlike that of an enraged rhino charging a Good Humor wagon. The antagonists surged to and fro, trampling shrubbery, shaking trees, grunting like beached walruses. Suddenly the stranger bent his knees, rammed his head into Smelch's midriff, and rose, Smelch spread-eagled across his shoulders. He pivoted sharply, went into a dizzying twirl, and hurled his unfortunate victim into the undergrowth, snapping off a medium-sized tree in the process. The victor paused only long enough to beat out a rapid tattoo on his chest and wait until a brief coughing fit passed before whirling on Retief. The Terran sidestepped the dimly seen monster's first rush, which carried the latter well into the thicket beside the path. As he threshed about there, roaring, Smelch reemerged from the opposite side of the route, shaking his head and muttering. The stranger came crashing back onto the scene only to be met by two lefts and a right haymaker that halted him in his tracks.

"Sorry about that, Retief," Smelch said contritely, as his antagonist toppled like a felled oak. "But the mug got my dander up, which he shouldn't ought to of came out leading with his chin anyways."

"A neat one-two-three," Retief commented, blowing a plume of smoke toward the fallen fighter. "Let's take a closer look." He parted the brush to look down at the casualty, who lay sprawled on his back, out cold. The ten-foot-tall figure was remarkably conservative for a Lumbagan, he thought: only two legs and arms, a single narrow head with close-set paired eyes, a lone nose and mouth, an unimpressive chin. The feet, clearly outlined inside rawhide buskins, featured five toes each, matching the hands' ten fingers.

"What's the matter?" Smelch said. "You know the mug?"

"No, but he bears a certain resemblance to a colleague of mine."

"Jeez, the poor guy. Well, beauty ain't everything. Anyways, here's your chance to pick up a set of dogs at a steal, if you know what I mean." He rammed an elbow toward Retief's ribs, a comradely gesture capable of collapsing a lung had it landed.

"I think I'll pass up the opportunity this time,"

Retief said, stepping forward to investigate a strand
of barbed wire vaguely discernible in the gloom. It
was one of three, he discovered, running parallel
to the trail, firmly attached to stout posts.

".Retief, we better blow," Smelch said. "Like
Flunt said, nobody but nobody don't want to poke
his noses and stuff in too close around you-know-
where."

"Actually, I don't think I do," Retief corrected
his massive acquaintance. "Know where, I mean."

"Good," Smelch said in a relieved tone. "You're
safer that way."

"Not afraid, are you?"

"Yeah. Smelch nodded his head vigorously. "I
hear they got ways of making a guy regret the day
his left leg met up with his right."

"Who says so?"

"Everybody, Retief! All the boys been warned to
stay clear, once they was outside. . . ."

"You mean you've been inside?"

"Sure." Smelch looked puzzled, an expression
involving a rapid twitching of his ears. "How could
I of not been?"

"Flunt's been there, too?"

"Natch. You don't figure the moomy-bird brung
him, do you? That's a little joke, Retief. I know
you know the moomy-bird didn't bring him."

"How about this fellow?" Retief indicated the
unconscious Lumbagan stretched at his feet. "He
came from inside, too?"

Smelch scratched at his chin. "I guess they must
of left out some o' your marbles, Retief. Where else
would Zung of come fron? In fact"—he lowered
his voice confidently—"he ain't graduated, poor
sucker."

"Maybe you'd care to amplify that remark a little, Smelch."

"Zung is one of the boys which they ain't been allowed out in the big, wonderful world like you and me." Smelch spread several hands expansively. "Except only maybe a few feet to clobber anybody that comes along. What I figure is...." He lowered his voice to a solemn hush. "Him and the other ones, they ain't all there, you know? Rejects, like."

"Rejects from what, Smelch?"

"Shhh." Smelch looked around worriedly. "I don't like the trend of the conversation, which we're treading on shaky ground, especially this close to you-know-what."

"No, but I think it's time I found out."

"Hey—you ain't planning on climbing the fence?"

"Unless you know where the gate is."

"Sure—right up the trail about a hundred yards, or maybe ten. I ain't too precise on the fine detail work."

"Then I'll be off, Smelch; give my regards to Flunt when you see him."

"You're really going to sneak back into you-know-where and grab a peek at you-know-what? Boy oh boy, if you-know-who sees us—"

"I know. Thanks for clarifying matters. By the way, if you should run into a fellow with three legs who answers to the name of Gloot, I'd appreciate any help you could give him."

"Sure. You let me know if we see him."

"We?"

"Heck, yes. You don't think I'm going in there alone, do you? And we better get moving. Zung's starting to twitch."

As they proceeded silently up the path, Retief was again aware of the soft rustlings and snufflings he had noted on and off since his arrival on the island. Through a gap in the shrubbery he caught a fleeting glimpse of a stealthy figure that ducked out of sight as he paused. He went on; the rustling progress of his shadower resumed.

The gate—a wide construction of aluminum panels and barbed wire—blocked the trail a hundred feet above the point where they had encountered Zung. A green-shaded spotlight outlined it starkly against the black foliage. A padlock the size of an alarm clock dangled from a massive hasp.

"Any more guards hidden out around the area?" Retief asked.

"Naw—with Flunt and me doing a tight security job down below, and the other bum working in close, who needs it?"

"An incisive point," Retief conceded. They walked boldly up to the gate. Smelch tried it, seemed surprised when it failed to swing open.

"Looks like it's stuck," he commented, and ripped it from its hinges, lock and all, tossing the crumpled panels aside with a metallic crash.

"Nothing like direct action," Retief said admiringly. "But from this point on I suggest we observe a trifle more caution, just in case there's anyone up there whose suspicions might be aroused by the sound of a three-car collision this far from the nearest highway."

"Say, pretty shrewd," Smelch said admiringly. "I always wanted to team up with a guy which he could figure the angles."

Beyond the former gate, the path continued a

few yards before debouching into a wide cleared strip adjoining a high board fence that extended for some distance in both directions.

"Home, sweet home," Smelch said nostalgically. "The old place sure has changed since I ventured out into the great world."

"Has it?"

"Sure. After all, that was a couple of hours ago."

"This is where you were born and raised, in other words."

"Yeah—inside the fence is where I spent my happy childhood, all four days of it."

"I'd like to see the old place."

"Well, old Sneakyfeet won't like it—but to heck with him and his dumb rules. Who but a alumnus would want to look inside anyways? Come on, Retief," Smelch led the way to an inconspicuous gate that yielded to his efforts, not without a certain amount of splintering. Retief propped the door back in place and turned to regard an extensive array of ranked cages stacked in long aisles that led away in the moonlight to the far line of the fence. A dispirited yammering chorus of sound started up nearby, reminiscent of visiting day at a pet hospital. A vaguely zoolike odor hung in the air.

Retief approached the nearest row of cages. In the first, a creature resembling a rubber rutabaga with spidery legs slumped dolefully against the bars. Adjacent, a pair of apprehensive-looking ankles huddled together for warmth.

"Freebies," Smelch said. "Just in from the jungle. Little do the poor little fellers dream what a high class destiny's in store for 'em."

"What destiny *is* in store for them, Smelch?"

"Right this way," the Lumbagan invited, indicating the next rank of cages. These were somewhat larger than those in the first section, each containing a creature giving the appearance of having been assembled from spare parts. Here a spindly leg drummed the fingers of a lone hand springing from where a foot might have been expected; there a bored-looking lower lip, flanked by a pair of generous ears, sprang directly from an unmistakable elbow. In the next echelon, the cages were still larger, occupied by specimens of a more sophisticated appearance. A well-developed paunch with a trio of staring brown eyes at the top squatted on four three-toed feet, watching the visitors incuriously. A remarkably human-looking head with a full beard swung from the roof of its prison by the muscular arm that was its sole appendage.

"Uh, at this stage, some o' the boys look a little weird," Smelch said apologetically, "but in the end they mostly turn out handsome devils, like me."

"Someone seems to have gone to considerable trouble to set up this lonelyhearts farm," Retief commented. "In the natural state, I understand, matches among Freebies take place at rare intervals. This looks like mass production. Any idea why, Smelch?"

"Nope. I ain't one of them guys which he asts questions all the time, you know what I mean? I mean, why poke the old nostrils in and maybe get 'em stuffed full of lint, right?"

"It's a philosophy without which bureaucracy as we know it would soon wither away," Retief conceded. "What was your job when you were here, Smelch?"

"Well, lessee, there was eating. That took a lot o' my time. Then there was sleeping. I liked that pretty good. Then ... lessee ... I guess that just about wraps it up. Why?"

"You must have a strong union," Retief said. "Why were you here?"

"Jeez, you know that's a question which a guy could wonder about it a long time if he wouldn't drop off to sleep first. Personally, I got like a theory that before we can attack the problem of transcendentalism, we got to examine the nature of knowledge and its limitations, making a appropriate distinction between *noumena* and *phenomena*. I figure by coordinating perceptions by means of rationally evolved concepts of understanding we can proceed to the analysis of experience and arrive at the categorical imperative, with its implicit concomitants. Get what I mean?"

"I think possibly I've been underestimating you, Smelch. I didn't know you read Kant."

"Can't read, you mean," Smelch corrected. "Nope, I never had the time for no idle pursuits, what with that heavy schedule I told you about."

"Quite understandable, Smelch. By the way, Flunt mentioned you'd only been here a week. Where were you before that?"

"Well, now we're getting into the area o' the metaphysical, Retief, which when you examine material phenomena by inductive processes you arrive at a philosophical materialism, not to exclude ontological and epistemological considerations, which in general could be assumed to deny metaphysics any validity in the context o' Aristotelian logic. Or am I just spinning my wheels?"

"Did you work that out for yourself, Smelch, or did somebody tip you off?"

"Never mind. I don't think I'd grasp the full significance of the answer anyway."

Foreword to an excerpt from
Time Trap

An ordinary man, propelled abruptly into a role in extraordinary affairs, perforce to do his best to discover who are the Good Guys and who the Bad, and then to do something effective about it, is an endlessly fruitful seed. Here, our victim/hero finds himself in a strange place only vaguely resembling our grade-school conception of early frontier America, but (who can say) perhaps more true-to-life than more conventional models, except for the Rhox, of course. If any double-entendre exists, it was entirely unintentional, but pretty neat, in spite of that.

An exerpt from
Time Trap

He awoke lying in a bed beside a hide-covered window aglow with watery daylight. A tall, gaunt, bearded man was standing over him, chewing his lower lip.

"Well, you're awake," Job Arkwright said. "Where was you headed anyways, stranger?"

"I . . . I . . . I . . ." Roger said. His hands and feet and nose hurt, but otherwise he seemed sound of wind and limb. "What happened? Who are you? How did I get here?" A sudden thought struck him. "Where is Mrs. Withers?"

"Your missus is all right. She's asleep." The gaunt man nodded toward a bunk above the one in which Roger lay.

"Say!" Roger sat bolt upright. "Are you the one that shot Luke?"

"Reckon so. Sorry about that. Friend o' yours, I s'pose. I took him for somebody else."

"Why?" Roger blurted.

"Reckon it was the bad light."

"I mean—why were you going to shoot somebody else?"

"Why, heck, I never even met your friend to talk to, much less shoot, leastwise on purpose."

"I mean—oh, never mind. Poor Luke. I wonder

what his last thoughts were, all alone out in the snow."

"Dunno. Why don't you ast him?" The stranger stepped back and Luke Harwood stood there, grinning down at Roger.

"B-but you're dead!" Roger yelped. "I saw you myself! There was a hole in you as big as your thumb!"

"Old Betsy's bite's as mean as her bark," Arkwright said proudly. "You should of seed Fly Beebody, time I picked him out of a pine at a hundred yards. One of my finest shots. He'll be along any minute now; get him to tell you about it."

"I told ye getting killed don't mean shucks," Luke said. "Job here done a clean job, never smarted a bit."

Roger flopped back with a groan. "I guess that means we're still stuck in the trap."

"Yes. But it could of been worse. At least Job here drug us inside out of the weather. I figger in your case, that saved yer skin."

There was a thumping at the door. A slim woman Roger hadn't noticed before opened it to admit a plump young fellow with a bundlesome overcoat and a resentful expression.

"The least thee could do, Brother Arkwright, would be to lay me out in Christian style after thee shoots me," he said past the woman as she took his coat and shook the snow from it.

"Don't like to see the remains cluttering up the place," Job said carelessly. "You ought to be thankful I let you in next morning."

"You mean—you actually shot that man?" Roger whispered hoarsely. "Intentionally?"

"Dern right. Caught him making up to Charity," he added in a lower tone. "Good cook, but flighty. And Fly's got a eye for the skinny ones. He goes along for a few days holding hisself under control, and then one day he busts loose and starts praising her corn meal mush, and I know it's time to teach him another lesson."

"How long has this been going on?"

"All winter. And it's been a blamed long winter, I'll tell you, stranger."

"Poor fellow! It must be ghastly for him!"

"Oh, I dummo. Sometimes he puts one over on me and gets me first. But he's a mighty poor shot. Plugged Charity once, by mistake, jist like I plugged your sidekick."

"Bloodcurdling!"

"Oh, Charity gets in her licks, too. She nailed the both of us once. Didn't care for it, though, she said afterward. Too lonesome. Now she alternates."

"You mean—she's likely to shoot you without notice—just like that?"

"Yep. But I calculate a man's got to put up with a few little quirks in a female."

"Good Lord!"

"Course, I don't much cotton to the idea of what goes on over my dead body—but I guess, long as she's a widder, it don't rightly count."

Charity Arkwright approached with a steaming bowl on a tray.

"Job, you go see to the kindling whilst I tend to this nice young man," she said, giving Roger a bright smile.

"Thanks, anyway," Roger said quickly, recoiling. "I'm allergic to all forms of gruel."

"Look here, stranger," Job growled. "Least you could do is try a little."

"I'm sure it's wonderful," Roger gulped. "I just don't want any."

"That sounds mighty like a slur to me, stranger!"

"No slur intended! It's just that I had a bad experience with my oatmeal as a child, and ever since I've been afraid to try again!"

"I bet I could help you with your problem," Charity offered, looking concerned. "The way I do it, it just melts in your mouth."

"Tell you what, Miz Charity," Luke Harwood put in. "I'll take a double helping—just to show ye ye're appreciated."

"Don't rush me, mister!" Charity said severely. "I'll get around to you when it's your turn!"

"Hey, stranger," Job said. "Your missus is awake; reckon she'd like some?"

"No! She hates the stuff!" Roger said, scrambling out of bed to find himself clad only in ill-fitting longjohns. "Give me my clothes! Luke, Mrs. Withers, let's get out of here!"

"Now, hold on, partner! You're the first variety we've had around this place in shucks knows how long! Don't go getting huffy jist over a little breakfast food!"

"It's not the food—it's the prospect of getting to know Betsy better. Besides which, we started out to find a way out of this maze, not just to settle down being snowbound!"

"I swan," Charity said. "And me the finest gruelmaker west of the Missouri! Never thought I'd see the day when I couldn't give it away!"

"Mister, I reckon you got a few things to learn about frontier hospitality," Job said grimly, lifting a wide-mouth muzzle-loader down from above the door and aiming it at Roger's chin. "I don't reckon nobody ain't leaving here until they've at least tried it."

"I'm convinced," Luke said.

"How do you like it?" Charity inquired. "Plain, or with sugar and cream?"

"Goodness, what's all this talk about gruel?" Mrs. Withers inquired from her bunk, sitting up. "I've got a good mind to show you my crepes suzettes."

"I never went in for none of them French specialties," Job said doubtfully. "But I could learn."

"Well, I like that!" Charity snapped. "I guess plain old country style's not good enough any more!"

"Well," Mrs. Withers said. "If it's all you can get . . ."

"Why, you scrawny little city sparrer!" Charity screeched, and leaped for the rival female. Roger yelled and lunged to intercept her. Job Arkwright's gun boomed like a cannon; the slug caught Charity under the ribs and hurled her across the room.

"Hey! I never meant—" That was as far as Arkwright got. The boom of a two-barreled derringer in the hands of Fly Beebody roared out. The blast knocked the bearded man backward against the door, which flew open under the impact, allowing him to pitch backward into the snow. As Roger staggered to his feet, a baroque shape loomed in the opening. Metallic tentacles rippled, bearing a rufous tuber shape, one-eyed, many-armed, into the cabin.

"Help!" Roger shouted.

"Saints preserve us!" Luke yelled.

"Beelzebub!" squealed Fly Beebody, and fired his second round into the alien body at point-blank range. The bullet struck with a fruity *smack!*, spattering carroty material; but the creature turned, apparently unaffected, and fixed its immense ocular on the parson. It rippled toward him, its grasping members outstretched.

Roger grabbed a massive hand-hewn chair, swung it up, and brought it down with tremendous force atop the blunt upper end of the monstrosity. It toppled under the blow, rolled in a short arc like an overturned milk bottle, threshed its tentacles briefly, and was still.

"Now will you leave?" Roger inquired in the silence.

"I'll go with thee!" Beebody yelped. "Satan has taken over this house in spite of my prayers!"

"We can't leave this thing here," Roger said. "We'll have to take it along; otherwise it will be the first thing to greet them in the morning!" He took a blanket from the bed, rolled the creature in it.

"Best ye stay here, girl," Luke said to Mrs. Withers. "Lord knows what we'll run into next."

"Stay here—with *them?*"

"They'll be themselves again tomorrow."

"That's what I'm afraid of!"

"Well, then; ye better don Charity's cloak."

"We'll leave the coats at the Aperture," Roger said. "In the morning, they'll be back here."

"I'll leave the can of soup," Mrs. Withers said as they prepared to step out into the sub-zero night. "I think Mr. Arkwright was getting a little tired of the same old gruel."

Outside, the wind struck at Roger's frost-nipped

face like a spiked board. He pulled his borrowed muffler up around his ears, hefted his end of the shrouded alien, and led the way up into the dark forest, following tracks made earlier that morning by Luke.

It was a fifteen minute hike through blowing snow to the spot among the trees where they had arrived. All of them except Beebody stripped off their heavy outer garments; Roger took the blanket-sack over his shoulder and held Mrs. Withers' hand, while Luke and Beebody joined to form a shivering line, like children playing a macabre game.

"Too bad we couldn't even leave them a note," Roger said. He approached the faint-glowing line, which widened, closed in about him, and opened out into brilliant sunlight on a beach of red sand.

Fly Beebody hunkered on his knees, his fingers interlaced, babbling prayers in a high, shrill voice. Luke stood staring around curiously. Mrs. Withers stood near him, still shivering, hugging herself. Roger dumped his burden at his feet, savoring the grateful heat. The sun, halfway to zenith, glared blindingly on choppy blue water, sand, and rock.

"No signs of life," Luke said. "Where would ye say we are, Roger?"

"That's hard to say. In the tropics, apparently. But what part of the tropics is as barren as this?"

He knelt, studied the sandy ground. "No weeds, no insects." He walked down across the loose sand to the water's edge, bent, and scooped up water in his hand and tasted it. It was curiously flat and insipid. No fish swam in the shallows, no moss grew on the rocks, no seaweed drifted on the tide.

"No seashells," he called. "Just a little green

scum on the water." As he turned to start back, he became suddenly aware of the sunlight beating down at him, the drag of gravity. He sucked air into his lungs, fighting a sense of suffocation that swept over him. Ahead, Fly Beebody's chanting had broken off; he half rose, bundlesome in the blanket coat, his mouth opening and closing like a fish's. Luke was struggling to support the widow, who sagged against him. Roger broke into a stumbling run.

"Back!" he called. "Get back through! Bad air!" He reached the group, caught the woman's limp hand.

"Grab Beebody's hand!" he gasped to Harwood. He caught up the bundle. As his vision began to fade into a whirling fog of flickering lights, he groped forward, found the Aperture, half-fell through it.

Foreword to an excerpt from
The House in November

There were four or five people in the car. Someone said: ". . . planning to build a house in November."

"Nice country around there," I commented, unnoticed, even by me. Later, at another place, I overheard the direction: ". . . turn left at the next opportunity."

"Are they clearly marked around here?" I inquired, receiving no answer. OK, if they wanna be that way, I'll just keep these gems to myself.

A second element entered into the genesis of The House in November: *When two people who know each other well sit down at a table and look at each other, what do they really* know *of the situation, past and present? Very little. This rather pretty woman with her hair in curlers could be an impostor, rung in by some unsuspected plotter for some unimaginable reason. Is that* really *nice, sanitary cornflakes in that box—or poison chips, or nothing at all? We take so much for granted.*

An excerpt from
The House in November

Jeff Mallory's first thought when he woke that morning was that he was back in the field hospital south of Inchon, with a hole in his shoulder where a Chinese .30 caliber slug had gone in, and a bigger one between his ribs where it had come out. And Uncle Al had been there, calling to him to come along: they were going to the Old House; and he had wanted to go, even though he was stitched and bandaged and confined to bed. . . .

Mallory moved his shoulders experimentally, felt a twinge of pain from sore muscles. Probably he had moved in his sleep and tried to weave the resultant ache into a dream that would allow him the luxury of a few more minutes of cosy oblivion. Strange thing, the dream mechanism: as if half the brain set out to delude the other half. And the haunting desire to see the Old House again still clung, like a memory of a long-ago outing. . . .

He got out of bed, stretched, noticing other small aches and pains as he did. Must be old age catching up with him, he told himself, not meaning it.

Through the curtained window, fog hung like a cottony veil across the lawn, making ghosts of the poplars at the far side of the garden, obscuring detail, blurring outlines, lending to the familiar a hint of the charm of the unknown. The Bartlett house, looming high and wraithlike beyond the trees, might have been perched on a cliff at the edge of the world. The street, dwindling into invisibility half a block away, might lead down to a silent beach edging a tideless sea. It would be pleasant to follow that phantom shoreline, wade in the warm, reed-grown shallows, emerge in some pleasanter, simpler. . . .

Mallory smiled at his fancies. It would be time enough to start dreaming of white beaches when the firm of Mallory and Nolan, Engineering Consultants, had weathered its first year in business.

As he turned away from the window, something caught his eye, lying beside the hedge lining the Bartletts' drive. It was difficult to make out in the misty light, but it looked like an old overcoat flung carelessly on the grass, a jarring note in the orderly composition. Probably something left and forgotten by a handyman. Mallory put it out of his mind and went into the bathroom.

His razor lay on the edge of the basin, clogged with gray soap. Bless the ladies, he thought as he rinsed it under the tap. He rummaged in the medicine cabinet for a new blade, failed to find one. The shaving cream can was empty, its spout crusted with dry, green foam. The toothpaste tube was crumpled and flat. His toothbrush was nowhere in sight. He found it after a brief search, on the floor behind the toilet bowl.

He used the electric razor Gill had given him for Christmas. He didn't like using it. It didn't shave close enough and left his face feeling dry and unrefreshed.

Eyeing himself in the mirror, he thought he

looked a bit gaunt and hollow-cheeked. There were dark semi-circles under his eyes, and he was badly in need of a haircut. That was at least a month's growth, he decided, angling his head to see the sides. He must be working too hard, losing weight, forgetting his biweekly trim. He'd have to think about taking things easier.

In the closet he noticed a pair of battered old shoes on the floor, belatedly realized it was his best pair of Bostonians. The shoes were badly worn, the uppers scuffed deep into the leather, the laces broken and knotted. Frowning, Mallory looked through the hanging clothes for his grey suit, found it dangling on a hook at the end of the closet. It was dusty, shabby, the cuffs greasy black, both elbows worn through. It looked, he thought, like something a hobo might wear, calling at the back door for a handout. Lori must have borrowed it, he decided, for some sort of student Rag Day or scavenger hunt thing. To a youngster, all old folks' clothes—meaning over 35—probably looked the same. He'd have to have words with that young lady.

He dropped the coat on the floor with the ruined shoes, selected a tan suit. His favorite tie was missing. He picked another, smoothed the frown off his face. Whistling, he went down to breakfast.

2

Gillian was at the stove, stirring a pan. Marly and Randy, the ten- and eight-year-olds, sat at the kitchen table, spooning up oatmeal.

"Looks like I'm last man on deck," Mallory said jovially. Gill smiled abstractedly and went on with her work. The kids didn't look up. He poured a cup of coffee and pulled out a chair. There were bread crumbs on the seat of the chair and on the table. Sugar was scattered around the bowl. In a clouded glass vase were the dried stems of a bunch of faded wildflowers. He tried the coffee. It was lukewarm, stale-tasting.

Gill came across and put a bowl of oatmeal before him. She was still the best-looking girl in town, Mallory thought, but this morning she looked pale, her skin dull.

"You're late, Jeff," she said. "I was just going to call you."

"I got involved in looking out the window," he said. "Nice fog."

Gill sat down across from him. "Fog?" she said vaguely.

Mallory glanced out the window. The air was sparkling clear.

"Funny; must have just been a patch."

He sampled the oatmeal. It was barely warm. There was no salt in it, no salt on the table, no butter, no cream. He started to mention it, glanced at Gill, noticed the darkness under eyes, her abstracted expression.

"Gill—are you feeling all right?"

"Very well, thank you," she said quickly, and smiled a fleeting smile.

Mallory got up and went to the cupboard where the dry cereal was kept. There were half a dozen boxes there, their tops torn open, all but one empty. He took a bowl from the shelf, noticed dust in it, rinsed it at the sink.

"Any toast?" he inquired.

"Toast?" Gill looked mildly puzzled.

"You've heard of it: bread that's been in the toaster." He tried to make it sound jolly, but the words hung dead between them. It was chilly in the room, he noticed. There was a faint, foul odor in the air. Or not so faint, he amended, noticing the overflowing garbage pail by the door. Bits of food and soiled paper lay around it.

Marly, the ten-year-old, scraped her spoon against her empty bowl. She licked it front and back, dropped it on the table, and stood. Her skirt and sweater didn't match.

"Hey, did you kids have any milk?" Jeff asked. Marly didn't answer. Randy pushed his chair back and started from the room after his sister.

"Why did the kids rush out of here without a word?" Mallory asked. "Is anything wrong?"

"They have to go to school," Gill said. She looked troubled. Mallory reached across to put his hand over hers. He was shocked at how cold it felt under his, and thin. And the nails, always so carefully groomed, were chipped, not even clean.

"Gill, what's the matter?" He tried to catch her eye. She looked down, into her bowl. She pulled her hand away, took a bite of gruel.

"Gill . . . I think you've been working too hard," Mallory said. "Being around the house too much. What do you say we get away for a few days? We could go out to the Old House this weekend, camp out, do a little work on the place. The kids would enjoy it and—"

"What old house?"

"*Our* Old House. What else?"

"Do we have an old house?" Gill looked at him innocently.

Mallory shook his head. "Never mind, it was just a thought."

"You'd better eat," Gill said. "You'll be late."

"One of the prerogatives of being boss," Mallory said, smiling, "is that I can be late when I want to."

Gillian shook her head. "You mustn't joke about your work, Jeff."

"Why not?" he smiled at her.

Gillian looked concerned.

"Jeff, you seem so strange this morning . . ."

"I was just thinking *you* seem to be in a curiously playful mood."

"In what way?"

"Acting as if you never heard of the Old House, teasing me about being a few minutes late to my own office—"

"Jeff, what are you talking about?"

"I'm talking about my business. Where I make our living."

"Jeff, are you sure you're feeling all right?"

"Why shouldn't I be?"

Gill's glance went to the clock over the refrigerator. She made as if to rise. "We really have to go now—"

Mallory caught her hand. "Where are you going?" She tugged against him, trying to pry his fingers loose.

"Let me go," she gasped. "They don't like it if you're late!"

"Gill—I asked you where you're going!"

"To the Star Tower, of course—"

"What's the Star Tower?"

"You know," she whispered. "It's where we work."

"We? Since when do *you* have a job?" He tried to smile. "I'm the breadwinner around here, remember?"

She was shaking her head. Her eyes were wide, fearful. Mallory came to his feet, drew his wife to him. "Slow down a minute, girl. Let's start at the beginning—" he broke off as the front door slammed. Through the window he saw Marly and Randy hurrying down the front walk.

"Where are their coats?" he said. "It's cold out there. And their school books—" He turned urgently to Gill.

"And where's Lori?"

"Lori who?"

"Our daughter, Lori. You know." He tried to cover the impatient edge to his voice with a smile.

"Our daughter's name is Marly," Gillian said carefully.

"Of course. And our other daughter's name is Lori. Has she already eaten?"

Gill gave him a fleeting half-smile. "I'm sorry, I don't understand you. I have to go. I mustn't be late to the workrooms."

"All right, I'll play along," Mallory said. "Anything else new I ought to know?"

Gillian looked worried. "Jeff, you know the quota has been increased—"

"Oh, so the quota has been increased." Mallory nodded solemnly.

"So many have not been coming to their benches."

"Their benches? What benches are those?"

"At the workrooms."

"What workrooms?"

"Where we work, of course, Jeff! Please stop—"

"Funny, I thought I had an office in the Miller Building," Mallory said harshly.

Gillian shook her head, glanced at the cereal bowl at Mallory's place. "You'd better eat quickly. It's a long time until midday break."

"Never mind the midday break. You still haven't said where Lori is."

"I don't know any Lori—"

He gripped her arm hard. "Stop it, Gill! Where is she—" He broke off at a sudden thought. "There hasn't been an accident? Has she been hurt?"

"No, there hasn't been any accident. And I don't know anyone named Lori." She tugged against him, trying to reach the door. He picked her up, carried her to the living room, lowered her to the couch. She tried to struggle up. He sat beside her, held her.

"There *has* been an accident, hasn't there?" He tried to hold his voice steady. "You're trying to keep it from me, aren't you?"

"I don't know what you mean! I have to go!" Gill tried to pull away. He drew her back.

"I'm talking about our eldest daughter, Lori," he said, forcing himself to speak calmly. "Age nineteen, born while we were still in school, tall, blonde, likes to ride and swim and play tennis. Are you telling me you've forgotten her?"

Gillian looked into his eyes, shaking her head.

"There isn't any such person, Jeff. We have two children, Marly and Randy. That's all!"

He rose, went into the hall and called. There was no answer. He ran up the stairs three at a time, at the top wheeled to the left, his outstretched hand reaching for the doorknob—

And slammed into a solid wall. Where the door to Lori's room should have been was an unbroken stretch of plaster.

Foreword to an excerpt from
Dinosaur Beach

When at work on a novel, I never know precisely what is going to happen next. I find it impossible to work to an outline, since invariably the characters and situation take on a life of their own, and go where they will. I usually know the final destination, but the route by which I arrive there is a matter of exploration. Dinosaur Beach is an extreme example: I had finished a long novel and was ready to begin a new one, and I wanted, as always, to enjoy writing it, which I accomplish by laying out a territory of speculation to explore: if a man finds himself in a strange situation, what does he do? As Raymond Chandler, a frustrated fantasist, said: "If a man woke up one morning and found he had turned into an elephant, I wouldn't be interested in how he got that way, but in what he was going to do about it."

Here, I began with an ordinary fellow sitting at a table in a dingy tavern, when a total stranger sits down opposite him. So, what happened then? I wrote

and discovered. First, I wrote a novelette, The
Timesweepers, *and later, reflecting on all the stones
I had left unturned, developed it into the novel. Here
is that germinal scene.*

An excerpt from
Dinosaur Beach

A streetcar clacked and sparked past the intersection. People hurried past, on their way home
after a long day. I bucked the tide, not hurrying,
not dawdling. I had plenty of time. That was one
lesson I'd learned. You can't speed it up, you can't
slow it down.

These reflections carried me the four blocks to
the taxi stand on Delaware. I climbed in the back
of a cab that looked as if it should have been
retired a decade back and told the man where I
wanted to go. "Make it under seven minutes and
there's five in it."

He dropped the flag and almost tore the clutch
out of the cab getting away from the curb. I saw
the neon letters half a block ahead and pulled him
over, shoved the five into his hand and was on my
way.

It was a shabby-genteel cocktail bar, with two
steps down into a room that had been a nice one
once, well before Prohibition. The maroon carpet
had a wide, worn strip that meandered like a jun-

gle trail across to the long bar, branching off to get
lost among the chair legs. The solid leather seats
in the booths along the wall had lost a lot of their
color, and nobody had bothered to polish away the
rings left by generations of beers on the oak
tabletops. I took a booth halfway back. The clock
over the bar said 7:44.

I ordered a grenadine from a waitress who'd
been in her prime about the same time as the bar.
She brought it and I took a sip and a man slid into
the seat across from me. He took a couple of breaths
and said, "Do you mind?"

I took my time looking him over. He had a soft,
round face, very pale blue eyes, the kind of head
that ought to be bald but was covered with a fine
blond down, like baby chicken feathers. He was
wearing a striped shirt and a bulky plaid jacket
with padded shoulders and wide lapels. His neck
was smooth-skinned, and too thin for his head.
The hand that was holding the glass was small
and well-lotioned, with short, immaculately mani-
cured nails. He wore a big, cumbersome-looking
gold ring with a glass ruby big enough for a paper-
weight on his left index finger. The whole composition looked a little out of tune, as if it had been put
together in a hurry.

"Please don't get the wrong impression," he said.
His voice was like the rest of him: not feminine
enough for a woman, but nothing you'd associate
with a room full of cigar smoke, either.

"It's vital that I speak to you, Mr. Ravel," he
went on, talking fast. "It's a matter of great impor-
tance . . . to your future."

He paused to check the effect of his words.

I said, "My future, eh? I wasn't sure I had one."

He liked that. "Oh, yes," he said, and nodded comfortably. "Yes, indeed." He caught and held my eyes, smiling an elusive little smile. "And I might add that your future is—or can be—a great deal larger than your past."

"I'm listening, Mr.—what was the name?"

"It really doesn't matter, Mr. Ravel. I don't enter into the matter at all except as the bearer of a message. I was assigned to contact you and deliver certain information."

"Assigned?"

He shrugged.

I reached across and caught the wrist of the hand that was holding the glass. It was as smooth and soft as a baby's. I applied a small amount of pressure. He tensed a little, as if he wanted to stand, but I pressed him back.

"Let me play, too," I said. "Let's go back to where you were telling me about your assignment. I find that sort of intriguing." He got his smile fixed up and back in place, a little bent now, but still working.

"Mr. Ravel—what would you say if I told you that I am a member of a secret organization of supermen?"

"What would you expect me to say?"

"That I'm insane," he said promptly. "That's why I'd hoped to skirt the subject and go directly to the point. Mr. Ravel, your life is in danger."

I let that hang in the air between us.

"In precisely"—he glanced down at his watch—"one and one-half minutes a man will enter this establishment. He will be dressed in a costume of black, and will carry a cane—ebony, with a silver head. He will go to the fourth stool at the bar, order a straight whisky, drink it, turn, raise the cane, and fire three lethal darts into your chest."

I took another swallow of my drink.

"Neat," I said. "What does he do for an encore?"

My little man looked a bit startled. "You jape, Mr. Ravel? I'm speaking of your death. Here. In a matter of seconds!"

"Well, I guess that's that," I said, and let go his arm and raised my glass to him. "Don't go spending a lot of money on a fancy funeral."

His fat little hand closed on my arm with more power than I'd given him credit for.

"Mr. Ravel—you must leave here at once." He fumbled in a pocket of his coat, brought out a card with an address printed on it: 356 Colvin Court.

"It's an old building, very stable, quite near here. There's an exterior wooden staircase, quite safe. Go to the third floor. A room marked with the numeral 9 is at the back. Enter the room and wait."

"Why should I do all that?" I asked him.

"In order to save your life!" He sounded a little wild now, as if things weren't working out quite right for him. That suited me fine. I had a distinct feeling that what was right for him might not be best for me and my big future.

"Where'd you get my name?" I asked him.

"Please—time is short. Won't you simply trust me?"

"The name's a phony," I said. "I gave it to a Bible salesman yesterday. Made it up on the spot."

His earnest look went all to pieces. He was still trying to reassemble it when the street door opened and a man in a black overcoat, black velvet collar,

black homburg, and carrying a black swagger stick
walked in.

"You see?" My new chum slid the whisper across
the table like a dirty picture. "Just as I said."

"Your technique is slipping," I said. "He had me
pat right down to my shoe size before he was
halfway through the door." I brushed his hand
away and slid out of the booth. The man in black
had gone across to the bar and taken the fourth
stool, without looking my way. I picked my way
between the tables and took the stool on his left.

He didn't look at me, not even when my elbow
brushed his side a little harder than strict eti-
quette allowed. If there was a gun in his pocket, I
couldn't feel it. I leaned a little toward him.

"Watch it, the caper's blown," I said about eight
inches from his ear.

He took it calmly. His head turned slowly until
it was facing me. He had a high, narrow forehead,
hollow cheeks, white lines around his nostrils
against grey skin. His eyes looked like little black
stones.

"Are you addressing me?" he said in a voice
with a chill like Scott's last camp on the icecap.

"Who is he?" I said.

"Who?" No thaw yet.

"The little guy I was sitting with. He's waiting
over in the booth to see how it turns out." I let
him have a sample of my frank and open smile.

"You've made an error," Blackie said, and turned
away.

"Don't feel bad," I said. "Nobody's perfect. The
way I see it, why don't we get together and talk it
over—the three of us?"

That got to him, his head jerked—about a mil-

lionth of an inch. My foot touched the cane as he
reached for it; it fell with a clatter. I accidentally
put a foot on it while picking it up for him. Something made a small crunching sound.

"Oops," I said, "sorry and all that," and handed
it over.

He grabbed it and headed for the men's room.
From the corner of my eye I saw my drinking
buddy sliding toward the street exit. I caught him
a few yards along the avenue, eased him over
against the wall. He fought as well as you can
fight when you don't want to attract the attention
of passers-by.

"Tell me things," I said. "After I bought the
mind-reading act, what was next?"

"You fool—you're not out of danger yet! I'm
trying to save your life—have you no sense of
gratitude?"

"If you only knew, chum. What makes it worth
the trouble?"

"Let me go! We must get off the street!" He tried
to kick my ankle, and I socked him under the ribs
hard enough to fold him against me wheezing like
a bagpipe. The weight made me take a quick step
back and I heart a flat *whup!* like a silenced pistol
and heard the whicker that a bullet makes when it
passes an inch from your ear. There was a deep
doorway a few feet away. We made it in one jump.

"Take it easy," I said. "That slug changes things.
Quiet down and I'll let go of your neck."

His round face looked a bit lopsided now, and
the China-blue eyes had lost their baby stare. I
made a little production of levering back the hammer of my Mauser, waiting for what came next.

Two or three minutes went past like geologic ages.

"He's gone," the little man said in a flat voice. "They'll chalk this up as an abort and try again. You've escaped nothing, merely postponed it."

"Sufficient unto the day and all that sort of thing." I nudged him forward with the gun. Nobody shot at him. I risked a look. No black overcoats in sight.

"Where's your car?" I asked. He nodded toward a black Marmon parked across the street. I walked him across and waited while he slid in under the wheel, then I got in the back.

"Any booze at your place?" I said.

"Why—yes—of course." He tried not to look pleased.

He drove badly, like a middle-aged widow after six lessons. We clashed gears and ran stoplights across town to a poorly-lit macadam dead end that rose steeply toward a tangle of telephone poles at the top. The house was tall and narrow, slanted against the sky. He led the way back along the side of the house, past the wooden steps he'd mentioned, used a key on a side door. It swung in on warped linoleum and the smell of last week's cabbage soup.

"Don't be concerned," the little man said. "There's no one here." He led me along a passage a little wider than my elbows, past a tarnished mirror, a stand full of furled umbrellas, and a hat tree with no hats, and up steep steps. We came out in a low-ceilinged hall with flowery brown wallpaper and dark-painted doors made visible by the pale light coming through a curtained window at the end.

He found number 9, opened up, and ushered me in.

It was a small bedroom with a hard-looking double bed, a brown wooden dresser with a string doily, a straight chair with wire to hold the legs together, a rocker that didn't match, an oval hooked rug in various shades of dried mud, and a hanging fixture in the center of the ceiling with three small bulbs, one of which worked.

"Just temporary quarters," he said off-handedly. He offered me the rocker and perched on the edge of the other chair.

"Now," he said, and put his fingertips together comfortably. "I suppose you want to hear all about the man in black."

"Not especially," I said. "What I'm wondering is what made you think you could get away with it."

"I'm afraid I don't quite understand," he said, and cocked his head sideways.

"It was a neat routine," I said. "Up to a point. After you fingered me, if I didn't buy the act, Blackie would plug me—with a dope dart. If I did, I'd be so grateful, I'd come here."

"As indeed you have." My little man looked less diffident now, more relaxed, less eager to please.

"Your mistake," I said, was in trying to work too many angles at once. What did you have in mind for Blackie—after?"

His face went stiff. "After—what?"

Foreword to
"The Devil You Don't"

From time to time, an idea pops into the mind of a writer, full-grown. This was one of mine: Hell is being invaded by alien demons from another world, so Old Nick comes to a scientist for help. After all, better the devil you know. . . .

By a curious coincidence, the kind I could never use to resolve a fictional plot, my friend and colleague, Anne McCaffrey, wrote me one day and told me she needed new stories for an anthology to be titled Alchemy in Academe. *I told her I had one in my head, awaiting the moment of creation, and here it is. I enjoyed writing it, which naturally involved analyzing the situation and discovering just what was involved. I was surprised at what came up, and have re-read it frequently, finding something new in it every time. Who would have thought that Maxwell's demon really existed?*

The Devil You Don't

Curlene Dimpleby was in the shower when the doorbell rang.

"Damn!" Curlene said. She did one more slow revolution with her face uptuned to the spray, then turned the big chrome knobs and stepped out onto the white nylon wall-to-wall, just installed that week. The full-length mirror, slightly misty, reflected soft curves nicely juxtaposed with slimness. She jiggled in a pleasant way as she toweled off her back, crossed the bedroom, pulled on an oversized white terry-cloth robe, and padded barefoot along the tiled hall to the front door. The bell rang again as she opened the door. A tall, wide, red-haired young man stood there, impeccably dressed in white flannels, a blue blazer with a fancy but somewhat tarnished pocket patch, and white buck shoes. He jerked his finger from the push button and smiled, an engaging display of china-white teeth.

"I'm . . . I'm sorry, ma'am," he said in a voice so deep Curlene imagined she could feel it through the soles of her feet. "I, uh . . . I thought maybe you didn't hear the bell." He stopped and blushed.

"Why, that's perfectly charming," Curlene said. "I mean, that's perfectly all right."

123

"Uh . . . I . . . came to fix the lights."

"Golly, I didn't even know they were out." She stepped back, and as he hesitated, she said, "Come on in. The fuse box is in the basement."

The big young man edged inside.

"Is, ah, is Professor Dimpleby here?" he asked doubtfully.

"He's still in class. Anyway, he wouldn't be much help. Johnny's pretty dumb about anything simple. But he's a whiz at quantum theory."

Curlene was looking at his empty hands.

"Possibly I'd better come back later?" he said.

"I notice," Curlene said reproachfully, "you don't have any tools."

"Oh—" This time the blush was of the furious variety. "Well, I think I'll just—"

"You got in under false pretenses," she said softly. "Gee, a nice looking fella like you. I should think you could get plenty of girls."

"Well, I—"

"Sit down," Curlene said gently. "How about a cup of coffee?"

"Thanks, I never tr—I don't care for . . . I mean I'd better go—"

"Do you smoke?"

He raised his arms and looked down at himself with a startled expression. Curlene laughed.

"Oh, sit down and tell me all about it."

The large young man swallowed.

"You're not a student, Mr. . . . ?" Curlene urged.

"No—not exactly—" He sat gingerly on the edge of a Danish chair. "Of course, one is always learning."

"I mean, did you ever think about going up to a coed and just asking her for a date?"

"Well, not exactly—"

"She'd probably jump at the chance. It's just that you're too shy, Mr. . . ?"

"Well, I suppose I am rather retiring, ma'am. But after all—"

"It's this crazy culture we live in. It puts some awful pressures on people. And all so needlessly. I mean what could be more natural—"

"Ah—when are you expecting Professor Dimpleby?" the young man cut in. He was blushing from neat white collar to widow's peak now.

"Oh, I'm embarrassing you. Sorry, I think I *will* get some coffee. Johnny's due back any time."

The coffee maker was plugged in and snorting gently to itself. Curlene hummed as she poured two cups, put them on a Japanese silver tray with creamer and sugar bowl. The young man jumped up as she came in.

"Oh, keep your seat." She put the tray on the ankle-high coffee table. "Cream and sugar?" She put his cup before him.

"Yes, with strawberries," the young man murmured. He seemed to be looking at her chin. "Or possibly rosebuds. Pink ones."

"They *are* nice, aren't they?" a booming male voice called from the arched entry to the hall. A tall man with tousled gray hair and a ruddy face was pulling off a scarf.

"Johnny, hi, home already?" Curlene smiled at her husband as she poured cream in the cups.

"The robe, Curl," Professor Dimpleby said. He gave the young man an apologetic grin. "Curl was raised in Samoa; her folks were missionaries, you know. She never quite grasped the concept that the female bosom is a secret."

Curlene tucked the robe up around her neck. "Golly," she said. "I'm sorry if I offended, Mr. . . ?"

"On the contrary," the young man said, rising and giving his host a slight bow. "Professor Dimpleby, my name is, er, Lucifer."

Dimpleby put out his hand. "Lucifer, hey? Nothing wrong with that. Means 'Light-bearer'. But it's not a name you run into very often. It takes some gumption to flaunt the old taboos."

"Mr. Lucifer came to fix the lights," Curlene said.

"Ah—not really," the young man said quickly. "Actually, I came to, er, ask for your help, Professor. Your help."

"Oh, really?" Dimpleby seated himself and stirred sugar into Curlene's cup and took a noisy sip. "Well, how can I be of service?"

"But first, before I impose on you any further, I need to be sure you understand that I really *am* Lucifer. I mean, I don't want to get by on false pretenses." He looked at Curlene anxiously. "I would have told you I wasn't really an electrician, er, Mrs.—"

"Just call me Curl. Sure you would have."

"If you say your name's Lucifer, why should I doubt it?" Dimpleby asked with a smile.

"Well, the point is—I'm *the* Lucifer. You know. The, er, the Devil."

Dimpleby raised his eyebrows. Curlene made a sound of distressed sympathy.

"Of course the latter designation has all sorts of negative connotations," Lucifer hurried on. "But I assure you most of what you've heard is grossly exaggerated. That is to say, I'm not really as bad as all that. I mean, there are different kinds of er, badness. There's the real evil, and then there's sin. I'm, ah, associated with sin."

"The distinction seems a subtle one, Mr., ah, Lucifer—"

"Not really, Professor. We all sense instinctively what true evil is. Sin is *statutory* evil— things that are wrong because there's a rule against them. Like, ah, smoking cigarettes and drinking liquor and going to movies on Sunday, or wearing lipstick and silk hose, or eating pork, or swatting flies, depending on which set of rules you're going by. They're corollaries to ritual virtues such as lighting candles or wearing out-of-date styles."

Dimpleby leaned back and steepled his fingers. "Hmmm. Whereas genuine evil . . . ?"

"Murder, violence, lying, cheating, theft," Lucifer enumerated. "Essentially, sin includes anything that looks like it might be fun."

"Come to think of it, I've never heard anything in praise of fun from the anti-sin people," Curl said thoughtfully.

"Not from any ecclesiastic with a good head for fund-raising," Dimpleby conceded.

"It's all due to human laziness, I'm afraid," Lucifer said sadly. "It seems so much easier and more convenient to observe a few ritual prohibitions than to actually give up normal business practices."

"Hey," Curlene said. "Let's not wander off into one of those academic discussions. What about you being—" she tittered "—the devil?"

"It's quite true."

"Prove it," Curlene said promptly.

"Well, er, how?" Lucifer inquired.

"Do something. You know, summon up a demon;

or transform pebbles into jewels; or give me three wishes; or—"

"Gosh, Mrs. Dimpleby—"

"Curl."

"Curl; you've got some erroneous preconceptions—"

"When they start using four-syllable words, I always know they're stalling," Curl said blandly.

Lucifer swallowed. "This isn't a good idea," he said. "Suppose somebody walked in?"

"They won't."

"Now, Curl, you're embarrassing our guest again," Dimpleby said mildly.

"No, it's all right, Professor," Lucifer said worriedly. "She's quite right. After all, I'm supposed to be a sort of, ahem, mythic figure. Why should she believe in me without proof?"

"Especially when you blush so easily," Curl said.

"Well . . ." Lucifer looked around the room. His eyes fell on the aquarium tank, which occupied several square feet of wall space under a bookcase. He nodded almost imperceptibly. Something flickered at the bottom of the tank. Curl jumped up and went over.

"The gravel," she gasped. "It looks different!"

"Diamond, ruby, emerald, and macaroni," Lucifer said. "Sorry about the macaroni. I'm out of practice."

"Do something else!" Curl smiled in eager expectation.

Lucifer frowned in concentration. He snapped his fingers and with a soft *blop!* a small, dark-purple, bulbous-bellied, wrinkle-skinned creature appeared in the center of the rug. He was some forty inches in height, with immense feet, totally naked, extravagantly male.

"Hey, for crying out loud, you could give a guy a little warning! I'm just getting ready to climb in the tub, yet!" The small being's bulging red eye fell on Lucifer. He grinned, showing a large crescent of teeth. "Oh, it's you, Nick! Howza boy? Long time no see. Anything I can do for ya?"

"Oops, sorry, Freddy," Lucifer snapped his fingers and the imp disappeared with a sharp *plop!*

"So that's a demon," Curl said. "How come his name is Freddy?"

"My apologies, Curl. He's usually most tastefully clad. Freddy is short for something longer."

"Know any more?"

"Er . . ." He pointed at Curl and made a quick flick of the wrist. In her place stood a tall, wide, huge-eyed coal-black woman in swirls of coarse, unevenly dyed cloth under which bare feet showed. Cheap-looking jewelry hung thick on her wrists, draped her vast bosom, winked on her tapered fingers and in her ears.

Lucifer flicked his fingers again, and a slim, olive-skinned girl with blue-black hair and a hooked nose replaced the buxom Sheban queen. She wore a skirt apparently made from an old guaze curtain and an ornate off-the-bosom vest of colored beads. A golden snake encircled her forehead.

Lucifer motioned again. The Egyptian empress dissolved into a nebulous cloud of pastel-colored gas in which clotted star-dust winked and writhed, to the accompaniment of massed voices humming nostalgic chords amid an odor of magnolia blossoms. Another gesture, and Curl stood again before them, looking slightly dazed.

"Hey, what was that last one?" she cried.

"Sorry, that was Scarlett O'Hara. I forgot she was a figment of the imagination. Those are always a little insubstantial."

"Remarkable," Dimpleby said. "I'll have to concede that you can either perform miracles or accomplish the same result by some other means."

"Gee, I guess you're genuine, all right," Curlene exclaimed. "But somehow I expected a much *older* man."

"I'm not actually a man, strictly speaking, ma'am—Curl. And agewise, well, since I'm immortal, why should I look middle-aged rather than just mature?"

"Tell me," Curlene said seriously. "I've always wondered: what do you want people's souls for?"

"Frankly, ma'am—Curl, that is—I haven't the remotest interest in anyone's soul."

"Really?"

"Really and truly, cross my heart. That's just another of those rumors *they* started."

"Are you sure you're really the Devil and not someone else with the same name?"

Lucifer spread his hands appealingly. "You saw Freddy. And those *are* noodles in the fish tank."

"But—no horns, no hooves, no tail—"

Lucifer sighed. "That idea comes from confusing me with Pan. Since he was a jolly sort of sex-god, naturally he became equated with sin."

"I've always wondered," Curlene said, "just what you did to get evicted from Heaven."

"Please," Lucifer said. "It . . . all dates back to an incident when I was still an angel." He held up a forestalling hand as Curl opened her mouth. "No, I *didn't* have wings. Humans added those when they saw us levitating, on the theory that anything that flies must have wings. If we were to appear today, they'd probably give us jets."

"Assuming you are, er, what you claim to be," Dimpleby said, "what's this about your needing help?"

"I do," Lucifer said. "Desperately. Frankly, I'm up against something I simply can't handle alone."

"I can't imagine what *I* could do, if you, with your, ah, special talents are helpless," Dimpleby said perplexedly.

"This is something totally unprecedented. It's a threat on a scale I can't begin to describe."

"Well, try," Curl urged.

"Stated in its simplest terms," Lucifer said, "the, ah, plane of existence I usually occupy—"

"Hell, you mean," Curl supplied.

"Well, that's another of those loaded terms. It really isn't a bad place at all, you know—"

"But what about it?" Dimpleby prompted. "What about Hell?"

"It's about to be invaded," Lucifer said solemnly. "By alien demons from another world."

2

It was an hour later. Lucifer, Curlene, and Professor Dimpleby were comfortably ensconced behind large pewter mugs of musty ale at a corner table in the Sam Johnson Room at the Faculty Club.

"Well, now," Dimpleby said affably, raising his tankard in salute, "alien demons, eh? An interesting concept, Mr. Lucifer. Tell us more."

"I've never believed in devils," Curlene said, "or monsters from another planet, either. Now all of a sudden I'm supposed to believe in both at once. If it weren't for that Freddy . . ."

"Granted the basic premise, it's logical enough," Dimpleby said. "If earthly imps exist, why not space sprites?"

"Professor, this is more than a bunch of syllogisms," Lucifer said earnestly. "These fellows mean business. They have some extremely potent powers. Fortunately, I have powers they don't know about, too; that's the only way I've held them in check so far—"

"You mean—they're already *here?*" Curlene looked searchingly about the room.

"No—I mean, yes, they're here, but not precisely *here,*" Lucifer clarified. "Look, I'd better fill in a little background for you. You see, Hell is actually a superior plane of existence—"

Curlene choked on her ale in a ladylike way.

"I mean—not *superior,* but, ah, at another level, you understand. Different physical laws, and so on—"

"Dirac levels," Dimpleby said, signaling for refills.

"Right!" Lucifer nodded eagerly. "There's an entire continuum of them, stretching away on both sides. There's an energy state higher on the scale than Hell—Heaven, it's called, for some reason—and one lower than your plane. That's the one Freddy comes from, by the way—"

"Oh, tell me about Heaven," Curlene urged.

Lucifer sighed. "Sometimes I miss the old place, in spite of . . . but never mind that."

"Tell me, Mr. Lucifer," Dimpleby said thoughtfully. "How is it you're able to travel at will among these levels?" As he spoke he pulled an envelope from his pocket and uncapped a ballpoint. "It appears to me that there's an insurmountable difficulty here, in terms of atomic and molecular spectral energy distribution; the specific heat involved . . ." He jotted busily, murmuring to himself.

"You're absolutely right, Professor," Lucifer said, sampling the fresh tankard just placed before him. "Heat used to be a real problem. I'd always arrive in a cloud of smoke and sulphur fumes. I finally solved it by working out a trick of emitting a packet of magnetic energy to carry off the excess."

"Hmmm. How did you go about dissipating this magnetism?"

"I fired it off in a tight beam; got rid of it."

"Beamed magnetism?" Dimpleby scribbled furiously. "Hmmm. Possibly . . ."

"Hey, fellas," Curlene protested. "Let's not talk shop, OK?" She turned a fascinated gaze on Lucifer. "You were just telling me about Heaven."

"You wouldn't like it, Curl," he said almost curtly. "Now, Professor, all through history—at least as far as I remember it, and that covers a considerable period—the different energy states were completely separate and self-sufficient. Then, a few thousand years back, one of our boys—Yahway, his name is—got to poking around and discovered a way to move around from one level to another. The first place he discovered was Hell. Well, he's something of a bluenose, frankly, and he didn't much like what he found there: all kinds of dead warriors from Greece and Norway and such places sitting around juicing it and singing, and fighting in a friendly sort of way."

"You mean—Valhalla really exists?" Curlene gasped. "And the Elysian fields?"

Lucifer made a disclaiming wave of the hand.

"There've always been humans with more than their share of vital energy. Instead of dying, they just switch levels. I have a private theory that there's a certain percentage of individuals in any level who really belong in the next one up—or down. Anyway, Yahway didn't like what he saw. He was always a great one for discipline, getting up early, regular calisthenics—you know. He tried telling these fellows the error of their ways, but they just laughed him off the podium. So he dropped down one more level, which put him here, a much simpler proposition, nothing but a few tribesmen herding goats. Naturally they were deeply impressed by a few simple miracles." Lucifer paused to quaff deeply. He sighed.

"Yes. Well, he's been meddling around down here ever since, and frankly—but I'm wandering." He hiccuped sternly. "I admit, I never could drink very much without losing my perspective. Where was I?"

"The invasion," Dimpleby reminded him.

"Oh, yes. Well, they hit us without any warning. There we were, just sitting around the mead hall taking it easy, or strolling in the gardens striking our lutes or whatever we felt like, when all of a sudden—" Lucifer shook his head bemusedly. "Professor, did you ever have one of those days when nothing seemed to go right?"

Dimpleby pursed his lips. "Hmmm. You mean like having the first flat tire in a year during the worst rainstorm of the year while on your way to the most important meeting of the year?"

"Or," Curlene said, "like when you're just having a quick martini to brace yourself for the afternoon and you spill it on your new frock and when you try to wash it out, the water's turned off, and when you try to phone to report *that*, the phone's out, and just then Mrs. Trundle from next door drops in to talk, only you're late for the Faculty Wives?"

"That's it," Lucifer confirmed. "Well, picture that sort of thing on a vast scale."

"That's rather depressing," Dimpleby said. "But what has it to do with the, er, invasion?"

"Everything!" Lucifer said, with a wave of his hands. Across the room, a well-fleshed matron yelped.

"My olive! It turned into a frog!"

"Remarkable," her table companion said. *"Rana pipiens,* I believe!"

"Sorry," Lucifer murmured, blushing, putting his hands under the table.

"You were saying, Mr. Lucifer?"

"It's them, Professor. They've been sort of leaking over, you see? Their influence, I mean." Lucifer started to wave his hands again, but caught himself and put them in his blazer pockets.

"Leaking over?"

"From Hell into this plane. You've been getting just a faint taste of it. You should see what's been going on in Hell, Proffefor—I mean Prossessor—I mean—"

"What *has* been going on?"

"Everything has been going to Hell," Lucifer said gloomily. "What I mean to say is," he said, making an effort to straighten up and focus properly, "that everything that *can* go wrong, *does* go wrong."

"That would appear to be contrary to the statistics of causality," Dimpleby said carefully.

"That's it, Professor! They're upsetting the laws

of chance! Now, in the old days, when a pair of our lads stepped outside for a little hearty sword-fighting between drinks, one would be a little drunker than the other, and he'd soon be out of it for the day, while the other chap reeled back inside to continue the party. Now, they each accidentally knee each other in the groin and they both lie around groaning until sundown, which upsets everybody. The same for the lute players and lovers: the strings break just at the climactic passage, or they accidentally pick a patch of poison ivy for their tryst, or possibly just a touch of diarrhea at the wrong moment—but you can imagine what it's doing to morale."

"Tsk," Dimpleby said. "Unfortunate—but it sounds more disconcerting than disastrous, candidly."

"You think so, Professor? What about when all the ambrosia on hand goes bad simultaneously, and the entire population is afflicted with stomach cramps and luminous spots before the eyes? What about a mix-up at the ferry that leaves us stuck with three boatloads of graduated Methodist ministers to entertain overnight? What about an extospheric storm that knocks out all psionics for a week, and has everyone fetching and carrying by hand, and communicating by sign language?"

"Well, that might be somewhat more serious—"

"Oh-oh!" Curlene was pointing with her nose. Her husband turned to see a waiter in weskit and knee-pants back through a swinging door balancing a tray laden with brimming port glasses, at the same moment that a tweedsy pedagogue rose directly behind him and, with a gallant gesture, drew out his fair companion's chair. There was a double *oof!* as they came together. The chair skidded. The lady sat on the floor. The tray distributed its burden in a bright cascade across the furs of a willowy brunette who yowled and whirled, causing her foxtail to slap the face of a small, elaborately mustached man who was on the point of lighting a cigar. As the match flared brightly, with a sharp odor of blazing wool, the tweedsy man bent swiftly to offer a chivalrous hand and, bumped by the rebounding waiter, delivered a smart rap with his nose to the corner of the table.

"My mustache!" the small man yelled.

"Dr. Thorndyke, you're bleeding on my navy-blue crepe!" the lady on the floor yelped. The waiter, still grabbing for the tray, bobbled it and sent it scaling through an olde English window, through which an indignant managerial head thrust in time to receive a glass of water intended for the burning mustache.

Lucifer, who had been staring dazedly at the rapid interplay, made a swift flick of the fingers. A second glass of water struck the small man squarely in the conflagration; the tweedsy man clapped a napkin over his nose and helped up the navy-blue crepe. The waiter recovered his tray and busied himself with the broken glass. The brunette whipped out a hanky and dabbed at her bodice, muttering. The tension subsided from the air.

"You see?" Lucifer said. "That was a small sample of their work."

"Nonsense, Mr. Lucifer," Dimpleby said, smiling amiably. "Nothing more than an accident—a curiously complex interplay of misadventures, true, but still—an accident, nothing more."

"Of course—but that sort of accident can only

occur when there's an imbalance in the randomness field!"

"What's that?"

"It's what makes the law of chance work. You know that if you flip a quarter a hundred times it will come up heads fifty times and tails fifty times, or very close to it. In a thousand tries, the ratio is even closer. Now, the coin knows nothing of its past performance—any more than metal filings in a magnetic field know which way the other filings are facing. But the field *forces* them to align parallel—and the randomness field forces the coin to follow the statistical distribution."

Dimpleby pulled at his chin. "In other words, entropy."

"If you prefer, Professor. But you've seen what happens when it's tampered with!"

"Why?" Dimpleby stabbed a finger at Lucifer and grinned as one who has scored a point. "Show me a motive for these hypothetical foreign fiends going to all that trouble just to meddle in human affairs!"

"They don't care a rap for human affairs," Lucifer groaned. "It's just a side effect. They consume energy from certain portions of the trans-Einsteinian spectrum, emit energy in other bands. The result is to disturb the R-field—just as sunspots disrupt the earth's magnetic field!"

"Fooey," Dimpleby said, sampling his ale. "Accidents have been happening since the dawn of time. And according to your own account, these interplanetary imps of yours have just arrived."

"Time scales differ between Hell and here," Lucifer said in tones of desperation. "The infiltration started two weeks ago, subjective Hell-time.

That's equal to a little under two hundred years local."

"What about all the coincidences before then?" Dimpleby came back swiftly.

"Certainly, there have always been a certain number of nonrandom occurrences. But in the last two centuries they've jumped to an unheard-of level! Think of all the fantastic scientific coincidences during that period, for example, such as the triple rediscovery of Mendel's work after thirty-five years of obscurity, or the simultaneous evolutionary theories of Darwin and Wallace, or the identical astronomical discoveries of—"

"Very well, I'll concede there've been some remarkable parallelisms." Dimpleby dismissed the argument with a wave of the hand. "But that hardly proves—"

"Professor, maybe that isn't what you'd call hard scientific proof, but logic—instinct—should tell you that Something's Been Happening! Certainly, there were isolated incidents in ancient history— but did you ever hear of the equivalent of a twenty-car pile-up in classical times? The very conception of slapstick comedy based on ludicrous accident was alien to the world until it began happening in real life!"

"I say again—fooey, Mr. Lucifer." Dimpleby drew on his ale, burped gently, and leaned forward challengingly. "I'm from New Hampshire," he said, wagging a finger. "You gotta show me."

"Fortunately for humanity, that's quite impossible," Lucifer said. "*They* haven't penetrated to this level yet. All you've gotten, as I said, is the spill-over effect—" he paused. "Unless you'd like to go to Hell and see for yourself—"

"No thanks. A faculty tea is close enough for me."

"In that case . . ." Lucifer broke off. His face paled. "Oh, no," he whispered.

"Lucifer—what is it?" Curlene whispered in alarm.

"They—they must have followed me! It never occurred to me, but—" Lucifer groaned. "Professor and Mrs. Dimpleby, I've done a terrible thing! I've led them here!"

"Where?" Curlene stared around the room eagerly.

Lucifer's eyes were fixed on the corner by the fire. He made a swift gesture with the finger of his left hand. Curlene gasped.

"Why, it looks just like a big stalk of broccoli—except for the eyes, of course—and the little one is a dead ringer for a rhubarb pie!"

"Hmmm." Dimpleby blinked. "Quite astonishing, really." He cast a sidelong glance at Lucifer. "Look here, old man, are you sure this isn't some sort of hypnotic effect?"

"If it is, it has the same effect as reality, Professor," the Devil whispered hoarsely. "And something has to be done about it, no matter what you call it."

"Yes—I suppose so—but why, if I may inquire, all this interest on your part in us petty mortals?" Dimpleby smiled knowledgeably. "Ah, I'll bet this is where the pitch for our souls comes in; you'll insure an end to bad luck and negative coincidences, in return for a couple of signatures written in blood—"

"Professor, please," Lucifer said, blushing. "You have the wrong idea completely."

"I just don't understand," Curlene sighed, gazing at Lucifer, "why such a nice fellow was kicked out of Heaven."

"But why come to *me?*" Dimpleby said, eyeing Lucifer through the sudsy glass bottom of his ale mug. "I don't know any spells for exorcising demons."

"Professor, I'm out of my depth," Lucifer said earnestly. "The old reliable eye-of-newt and wart-of-toad recipes don't faze these alien imps for a moment. Now, I admit, I haven't kept in touch with new developments in science as I should have. But *you* have, Professor: you're one of the world's foremost authorities on wave mechanics and Planck's law, and all that sort of thing. If anybody can deal with these chaps, *you* can!"

"Why, Johnny, how exciting!" Curlene said. "I didn't know matrix mechanics had anything to do with broccoli!" She took a pleased gulp of ale, smiling from Lucifer to her husband.

"I didn't either, my dear," Dimpleby said in a puzzled tone. "Look here, Lucifer, are you sure you don't have me confused with our Professor Pronko, over in Liberal Arts? Now, his papers on abnormal psychology—"

"Professor, there's been no mistake! Who else but an expert in quantum theory could deal with a situation like this?"

"Well, I suppose there is a certain superficial semantic parallelism—"

"Wonderful, Professor, I knew you'd do it!" Lucifer grabbed Dimpleby's hand and wrung it warmly. "How do we begin?"

"Here, you're talking nonsense!" Dimpleby extracted his hand, used it to lift his ale tankard once again.

"Of course," he said after taking a hearty pull, "if you're right about the nature of these varying energy levels—and these, er, entities *do* manage the jump from one quantum state to the next— then I suppose they'd be subject to the same sort of physical laws as any other energetic particles ..." He thumped the mug down heavily on the table-top and resumed jotting. "The Compton effect," he muttered. "Raman's work . . . the Stern-Gerlack experiment. Hmmm."

"You've got something?" Lucifer and Curlene said simultaneously. "Just a theoretical notion," Dimpleby said offhandedly, and waved airily to a passing waiter. "Three more, Chudley."

"Johnny," Curlene wailed. "Don't stop now!"

"Professor—time is of the essence!" Lucifer groaned.

"Say, the broccoli is stirring around," Curlene said in a low tone. "Is he planning another practical joke?"

Lucifer cast apprehensive eyes toward the fire-place. "He doesn't actually do it intentionally, you know. He can't help it; it's like, well, a blind man switching on the lights in a darkroom. He wouldn't understand what all the excitement was about."

"Excuse me," Dimpleby said. "Ale goes through me pretty rapidly." He rose, slightly jogging the elbow of the waiter pouring ice water into a glass at the next table. The chilly stream dived precisely into the cleavage of a plump woman in a hat like a chef's salad for twelve. She screamed and fell back-ward into the path of the servitor approaching with a tray of foaming ale tankards. All three malt beverages leaped head-first onto the table, their contents sluicing across it into Lucifer's lap, while the overspill distributed itself between Dimpleby's hip pockets.

He stared down at the table awash in ale, turned a hard gaze on the fireplace.

"Like that, eh?" he said in a brittle voice. He faced the Devil, who was dabbing helplessly at his formerly white flannels.

"All right, Lucifer," he said. "You're on! A few laughs at the expense of academic dignity are fine, but I'm damned if I'm going to stand by and see good beer wasted! Now, let's get down to cases. Tell me all you know about these out-of-town incubi . . ."

3

It was almost dawn. In his third-floor laboratory in Prudfrock Hall, Professor Dimpleby straightened from the marble-topped bench over which he had been bent for the better part of the night.

"Well," he said rubbing his eyes, "I don't know. It might work." He glanced about the big room. "Now, if you'll just shoo one of your, ah, extraterrestrial essences in here, we'll see."

"No problem there, Professor," Lucifer said anxiously. "I've had all I could do to hold them at bay all night, with some of the most potent incantations since Solomon sealed the Afrit up in a bottle."

"Then, too, I don't suppose they'd find the atmosphere of a scientific laboratory very congenial," Dimpleby said with a somewhat lofty smile, "inasmuch as considerable effort has been devoted to excluding chance from the premises."

"You think so?" Lucifer said glumly. "For your

own peace of mind, I suggest you don't conduct any statistical analyses just now."

"Well, with the clear light of morning and the dissipation of the alcohol, the rationality of what we're doing seems increasingly questionable," the professor said, "but nonetheless, we may as well carry the experiment through. Even negative evidence has a certain value."

"Ready?" Lucifer said.

"Ready," Dimpleby said, suppressing a yawn. Lucifer made a face and executed an intricate dance step. There was a sharp sense of tension released— like the popping of an invisible soap bubble—and *something* appeared, drifting lazily in the air near the precision scales. One side of the instrument dropped with a sharp *clunk!*

"All the air concentrated on one side of the balance," Lucifer said tensely.

"Maxwell's demon—in the flesh?" Dimpleby gasped.

"It looks like a giant pizza," Curlene said, "only transparent."

The apparition gave a flick of its rim and sailed across to hover before a wall chart illustrating the periodic table. The paper burst into flame.

"All the energetic air molecules rushed to one spot," Lucifer explained. "It could happen any time— but it seldom does."

"Good Lord! What if it should cause all the air to rush to one end of the room?" Dimpleby whispered.

"I daresay it would rupture your lungs, Professor. So I wouldn't waste any more time, if I were you."

"Imagine what must be going on outside," Curlene said. "With these magical pizzas and broccoli wandering loose all over the place!"

"Is *that* what all those sirens were about?" Dimpleby said. He stationed himself beside the breadboard apparatus he had constructed and swallowed hard.

"Very well, Lucifer—see if you can herd it over this way."

The devil frowned in concentration. The pizza drifted slowly, rotating as if looking for the source of some irritation. It gave an impatient twitch and headed toward Curlene. Lucifer made a gesture and it veered off, came sailing in across the table.

"Now!" Dimpleby said, and threw a switch. As if struck by a falling brick, the alien entity slammed to the center of the three-foot disk, encircled by massive magnetic coils. It hopped and threshed, to no avail.

"The field is holding it!" Dimpleby said tensely. "So far . . ."

Suddenly the rippling, disk-shaped creature folded in on itself, stood on end, sprouted wings and a tail. Scales glittered along its sides. A puff of smoke issued from tiny crocodilian jaws, followed by a tongue of flame.

"A dragon!" Curlene cried.

"Hold him, Professor!" Lucifer urged.

The dragon coiled its tail around itself and melted into a lumpy black sphere covered with long bristles. It had two bright red eyes and a pair of spindly legs on which it jittered wildly.

"A goblin?" Dimpleby said incredulously.

The goblin rebounded from the invisible wall restraining it, coalesced into a foot-high, leathery-skinned humanoid with big ears, a wide mouth, and long arms which it wrapped around its knees as it squatted disconsolately on the grid, rolling bloodshot eyes sorrowfully up at its audience.

"Congratulations, Professor!" Lucifer exclaimed. "We got one!"

4

"His name," Lucifer said, "is Quilchik. It's really quite a heart-rending tale he tells, poor chap."

"Oh, the poor little guy," Curlene said. "What does he eat, Mr. Lucifer? Do you suppose he'd like a little lettuce, or something?"

"His diet is quite immaterial, Curl; he subsists entirely on energies. And that seems to be at the root of the problem. It appears there's a famine back home. What with a rising birth rate and no death rate, population pressure long ago drove his people out into space. They've been wandering around out there for epochs, with just the occasional hydrogen molecule to generate a quantum or two of entropy to absorb; hardly enough to keep him going."

"Hmmm. I suppose entropy *could* be considered a property of matter," Dimpleby said thoughtfully, reaching for paper and pencil. "One can hardly visualize a distinction between order and disorder as existing in matterless space."

"Quite right. The curious distribution of heavy elements in planetary crusts and the unlikely advent of life seem to be the results of their upsetting of the randomness field, to say nothing of evolution, biological mutations, the extinction of the dinosaurs just in time for man to thrive, and women's styles."

"Women's styles?" Curlene frowned.

"Of course," Dimpleby nodded. "What could be more unlikely than this year's Paris modes?"

Lucifer shook his head, a worried expression on his regular features. "I had in mind trapping them at the entry point and sending them back where they came from; but under the circumstances that seems quite inhumane."

"Still—we can't let them come swarming in to upset everything from the rhythm method to the Irish Sweepstakes."

"Golly," Curlene said, "couldn't we put them on a reservation, sort of, and have them weave blankets, maybe?"

"Hold it," Lucifer said. "There's another one nearby. I can feel the tension in the R-field . . ."

"Eek!" Curlene said, taking a step backward and hooking a heel in the extension cord powering the magnetic fields. With a sharp *pop!* the plug was jerked from the wall. Quilchik jumped to his large, flat feet, took a swift look around, and leaped, changing in midair to the fluttering form of a small bat.

Lucifer threw off his coat, ripped off his tie and shirt. Before the startled gaze of the Dimplebys, he rippled and flowed into the form of a pterodactyl, leaped clear of the collapsing white flannels and into the air, long beak agape, in hot pursuit of the bat. Curlene screeched and squeezed her eyes shut. Dimpleby said: "Remarkable!" grabbed his pad, and scribbled rapidly. The bat flickered in midair and was a winged snake. Lucifer turned instantly into a winged mongoose. The snake dropped to the floor and shrank to mouse form, scuttling for a hole. Lucifer became a big gray cat, reached the hole first. The mouse burgeoned into a bristly rat;

the cat swelled and was a terrier. With a yap, it leaped after the rat, which turned back into Quilchik, sprang up on a table, raced across it, dived for what looked like an empty picture frame—

A shower of tiny Quilchiks shot from the other side of the heavy glass sheet. Lucifer barely skidded aside in time to avoid it, went dashing around the room, barking furiously at the tiny creatures crouched behind every chair and table leg, squeezing in behind filing cabinets, cowering under ashtrays.

"Lucifer, stop!" Curlene squealed. "Oh, aren't they *darling!*" She went to her knees, scooped up an inch-high manikin. It squatted on her palm, trembling, its head between its knees.

"By Jiminy," Dimpleby said. "It went through a diffraction grating, and came out centuplets!"

5

"The situation is deteriorating," Lucifer groaned, scooping up another miniature imp and dumping it back inside the reactivated trap. "It was bad enough dealing with one star-sprite. Now we have a hundred. And if any one of them escapes . . ."

"Don't look now," Dimpleby said behind his hand to the Devil, now back in human form and properly clad, "but I have an unch-hay the magnetic ield-fay won't old-hay em-they."

"Eye-way ott-nay?" Lucifer inquired.

"Ecause-bay . . ." Dimpleby broke off. "Well, it has to do with distribution of polarity. You see, the way the field works—"

"Don't bother explaining," Lucifer said. "I

wouldn't understand anyway. The real question is—what do we do now?"

"Our choice seems limited. We either gather up all these little fellows and dump them back where they came from, and then hunt down the others and do likewise, which is impossible, or we forget the whole thing, which is unthinkable."

"In any event," Lucifer said, "we have to act fast before the situation gets entirely out of hand."

"We could turn the problem over to the so-called authorities," Dimpleby said. "But that seems unwise, somehow."

Lucifer shuddered. "I can see the headlines now: DEVIL LOOSE ON COLLEGE CAMPUS!"

"Oh, they've already worked that one to death," Curlene said. "It would probably be more like: PROF AND MATE IN THREE-WAY SEX ROMP."

"Sex romp?"

"Well, Mr. Lucifer *did* reappear in the nude." Curlene smiled. "And a very nice physique, too, Mr. Lucifer."

Lucifer blushed. "Well, Professor, what do we do?" he asked hastily.

"I'll flip a coin," Curlene suggested. "Heads, we report the whole thing, tails, we keep it to ourselves and do the best we can."

"All right. Best two of three."

Curlene rummaged in her purse and produced one of the counterfeit quarters in current production from the Denver mint. She tossed it up, caught it, slapped it against her forearm, lifted her hand.

"Tails," she said in a pleased tone.

"Maybe we'd better report it anyway," Dimpleby said, nibbling a fingernail and eyeing the tiny creatures sitting disconsolately inside the circle of magnets.

"Two out of three," Curlene said. She flipped the coin up.

"Tails again," she announced.

"Well, I suppose that settles it . . ."

Curlene tossed the coin up idly. "I guess it's definite," she said. "Tails three times in a row."

Dimpleby looked at her absently. "Eh?"

"Four times in a row," Curlene said. Lucifer looked at her as if about to speak. Curlene flipped the coin high.

"Five," she said. Dimpleby and Lucifer drew closer.

"Six . . ."

"Seven . . ."

"Eight . . ."

"Oh-oh," Dimpleby said. He grabbed for the desk drawer, pulled out a dog-eared deck of cards, hastily shuffled and dealt two hands. Cautiously, he peeked at his cards. He groaned.

"Four aces," he said.

"Four kings here," Curlene said.

"Here we go again," he said. "Now no one will be safe!"

"But Johnny," Curlene said. "There's one difference."

"What?"

"The odds are all mixed up, true—but now they're in our favor!"

6

"It's quite simple, really," Dimpleby said, waving a sheet of calculation. "When Quilchik went through the grating, he was broken up into a set of

harmonics. Those harmonics, being of another order of size, resonate at another frequency. Ergo, he
consumes a different type of energetic pseudo-
particle. Instead of draining off the positive, ah,
R-charges, he now subsists on negative entropy."

"And instead of practical jokes, we have miraculous cures, spontaneous remissions, and fantastic
runs with the cards!" Curlene cried happily.

"Not only that," Dimpleby added, "but I think
we can solve their food-supply problem. They've
exhausted the supply of plus entropy back on
their own level—but the original endowment of
minus-R remains untapped. There should be enough
for another few billion years."

Lucifer explained this to the Quilchiks via the
same form of instantaneous telepathy he had employed for the earlier interrogation.

"He's delighted," the Devil reported, as the tiny
creatures leaped up, joined hands, and began ca-
pering and jiggling in a manner expressive of joy.
"There's just one thing . . ." A lone manikin stood
at the edge of the table, looking shyly at Curlene.

"Quilchik Seventy-eight has a request," Lucifer
said.

"Well, what does snookums-ookums want?"
Curlene cooed, bending over to purse her lips at
the tiny figure.

"He wants to stay," Lucifer said embarrassedly.

"Oh, Johnny, can I have him?"

"Well—if you'll put some pants on him . . ."

"And he'd like to live in a bottle. Preferably a
bourbon bottle, one of the miniatures. Preferably
still full of bourbon," Lucifer added. "But he'll
come out to play whenever you like."

"I wonder," Dimpleby said thoughtfully, "what

effect having him around would have on the regular Saturday-night card game with those sharpies from the Engineering faculty?"

"You've already seen a sample," Lucifer said. "But I can ask him to fast at such times."

"Oh, no, no," Dimpleby protested. "Hate to see the little fellow go hungry."

"Mr. Lucifer," Curlene asked. "I hope I'm not being nosy—but how did you get the scar on your side that I saw when you had your shirt off?"

"Oh, ah, that?" Lucifer blushed purple. "Well, it, ah—"

"Probably a liver operation, from the location, eh, Lucifer?" Dimpleby said.

"You might call it that," Lucifer said.

"But you shouldn't embarrass people by asking personal questions, Curl," Dimpleby said sternly.

"Yes, dear," Curl said. "Lucifer—I've been wanting to ask you: what did a nice fellow like you do to get kicked out of Heaven?"

"Well, I, uh," Lucifer swallowed.

"It was for doing something nice, wasn't it?"

"Well—frankly, I thought it wasn't fair," Lucifer blurted. "I felt sorry for the poor humans, squatting in those damp caves . . ."

"So you brought them fire," Curlene said. "That's why you're called Lucifer."

"You're mixed up, Curl," Dimpleby said. "That was Prometheus. For his pains, he was chained to a rock, and every day a vulture tore out his liver, and every night it grew back . . ."

"But it left a scar," Curlene said, looking meltingly at Lucifer.

The Devil blushed a deep magneta. "I . . . I'd better be rushing off now," he said.

"Not before we share a stirrup cut," Dimpleby said, holding up the Old Crow bottle from the desk drawer. Inside, Quilchik, floating on his back with his hands folded on his paunch, waved merrily and blew a string of bubbles.

"Luckily, I have a reserve stock," Dimpleby muttered, heading for the filing cabinet.

"Mr. Lucifer, how can we ever thank you?" Curlene sighed, cradling the flask.

"Just by, uh, having all the fun you can," Lucifer said. "And I'll, er, be looking forward to seeing you in Hell, someday."

"I'll drink to that," Dimpleby said. He poured. Smiling, they clicked glasses and drank.

Foreword to an excerpt from
The Ultimax Man

Mankind as a whole has mastered many diverse talents, though an individual never becomes expert in more than a very few. Suppose many widely divergent talents were imparted to a single man? How much could he absorb? Could he learn to dance like Fred Astaire and to sing like Pavarotti (and at the same time theorize like Einstein and fight like Muhammed Ali)? And if he did, what serendipitous abilities might arise from this unheard-of exercise of the psyche?

There is more than one way in which a plain man might accumulate vast stores of knowledge.

I had nearly completed the The Ultimax Man before I realized who he was.

An excerpt from
The Ultimax Man

"I guess arenas are all the same, from the Circus Maximus to Yankee Stadium," Danny reflected as he surveyed the structure looming above him. The noisemakers strutted, making noises. Banners rippled in a light breeze.

A pair of iron gates at the far side of the arena opened with a clang. Two Trismans with long poles stood by alertly as something came charging from the dark tunnel under the grandstand, plantigrade on four awkward limbs.

At first glimpse, Dammy thought it was a bear. Then, "Nope," he decided, "too skinny, and—"

Next, as the galloping creature slid to a halt and crouched, then sprawled, its dark, shaggy pelt dust-splotched, it seemed to be a man wearing fur longjohns.

Dammy advanced cautiously. When he was 10 feet from the beast, it stirred; long arms and bowed legs disconcertingly terminating in almost human hands stretched. One foot reached across to scratch with black-nailed fingers at a threadbare patch that Dammy now saw was a less densely furred chest. The creature rolled over onto its back. At the head end, an astonishingly wide mouth opened on large, squarish, lemon-yellow teeth and a bright pink buccal cavity, where a grayish tongue lolled. Above the mouth were two orifices nearly an inch in diameter, surrounded by whorls and convolutions of what appeared to be gristly black flesh. Still higher, a pair of small, red-edged, and bloodshot brown eyes stared back at him blandly.

"Hey," Dammy said. "It's some kind of big monkey or something. But it has hominid 5-Y dentition. . . ."

Astonishing, a clear but silent voice spoke between Dammy's ears. *Such a freak as this, seeing me in my beauty as a kind of overgrown meepa. It is of the people by its smell, but far gone in sickness, its body bald, its limbs somewhat wasted. It has covered itself in strange skins to hide the shameful disease. But what the hell—company's company.*

Gee, thanks, pal, Dammy thought sardonically. *I guess I'm really in the big time now, being accepted as one of the boys by an overgrown rhesus. Or maybe Australopithecus robustus, to be technical.*

"Hi," he said aloud. The apelike man-thing recoiled and rolled its eyes as if searching for an escape route.

It barked at me, the creature's thought came clearly to Dammy. *I hope it doesn't attack. . . .* The creature extended four empty hands one by one in a tentative way. Dammy gently shook each in turn. The horny palms felt hot and dry and hard, like a dog's paw. The ape-man took this gesture in good part, looking more cheerful now.

"Don't worry, sport," Dammy said soothingly. "I promise not to bite first."

Curious. Sport's reaction came to Dammy not precisely as silent words, but as wordless concepts.

It barks as it speaks. One wonders why. Why do you bark, fellow?

"Well, I'll tell you, Sport," Dammy said softly. "It's the practice back home these days. By the way, how long have you been in stir?"

Based on the residual percentage of nuclide 152 I note in my tissues, I estimate . . . um, may I rummage for a unit of measure? Dammy winced as he felt the ghostly touch inside his skull.

"That's the first time anybody but me ever racked my memory," he commented.

Ah, here we are . . . one million, seven hundred and forty-two thousand, nine hundred and four and one-half, uh, years.

"Almost two million years?" Dammy gasped. "How come you're not dead, Sport?"

I'm a philosophical sort of fellow, I suppose, Sport replied. *I go along from sleep to sleep, meal to meal, getting what pleasure I can from life—and somehow it hasn't yet seemed necessary to terminate.*

"You sound like it was up to you," Dammy said weakly.

I can hardly catch your speech, for your barking, Sport said. *Why not discontinue the barking and let's have a quiet talk, there's a good fellow. And of course it's up to me—what else?*

"Where I come from, most guys live as long as they can, and then they go kicking and screaming."

Seems dreadful, Sport commented. *And where do you come from?*

"How's your astronomy?" Dammy asked bluntly.

Poor. I doubt that I could enumerate the spectral characteristics of more than half the stars in this Galaxy alone.

"I see. Well, here it is." Dammy visualized the

location of Sol relative to 61 Cygni, Alpha Centauri,
Vega, Capella, Sirius, etc.

Remarkable! Sport commented. *Actually . . . but
no, that's unlikely. Still, yes, the Star of the Cold
Bride, and the double planet itself! Come to my arms,
fellow, diseased or no! We are, it seems, planet-fellows.*

Dammy accepted the man-thing's embrace without enthusiasm.

You hung back, Sport noted. *You're shy—but don't
feel inferior, simply because of a physical circum-
stance. But stay! I can show you quite easily how to
re-stimulate the old follicles, and we'll have you as
handsome as myself in a trice!*

"Never mind, Sport," Dammy declined. "It's a
friendly thought and it does you credit. But I'm
saving my strength for the crunch."

You anticipate difficulties? Sport inquired without urgency.

"I've already *got* difficulties," Dammy pointed
out. "How about you, Sport? You like being cooped
up for two million years?"

You exaggerate, Sport demurred. *Actually I've seen
a great deal more of the Galaxy than I would have
turning over rotted logs looking for succulent grubs
back in good old Here.*

"You're not one of those optimists, are you?"
Dammy demanded.

A curious thought, Sport responded. *How can
one 'look on the bright side,' when every side is so
bright?*

"I've been trying to figure out what species you
are," Dammy confided in Sport. "No doubt about
your being Animalia, Chordata, Vertebrata, Mam-
malia, Eutheria, Primata, Anthropoidiae, but after
that it looks kind of dubious. No offense, but

nobody's ever dug up a Hominidea with hands on his leg bones."

Umm. Actually, I shouldn't expect the metatarsals would fossilize all that well, was Sport's only comment.

"Two million years," Dammy mused. "That would put you back in the time of Australopithecus." He visualized the latter as reconstructed.

Oh, those *little fellows. Had one chap who caught a young female and claimed he was keeping her as a pet; then one day she turned up preggers. So they must be a closely related species, though one hates to acknowledge it.*

"May I?" Dammy inquired, and extended a sensory feeler to explore Sport's cerebrum.

Go right ahead. I've already studied you, rather rudely, I admit, while you were busy thinking of other matters. Silently Dammy nodded and proceeded to examine Sport's cortex.

"This is kind of strange," he commented. "Broca's and Wernicke's areas both hypertrophied, and the angular gyrus undersized. I assume that's got something to do with your being a telepath. . . ." He probed further and was astonished to discover an anterior extension of the arcuate fasciculum to a well-developed patch of the cortex for which no specific function was known.

"We're wired up a bit differently," he told his cellmate. "But I guess you wouldn't know much about anatomy."

No more than I do of astronomy. I noticed your curiously withered speech areas, and I assume the oddly truncated fasciculum is responsible for your odd habit of barking as you speak.

"Funny idea," Dammy replied. "Early man was

telepathic, and evolved away from it. I wonder why?"

Perhaps I can explain that, Sport offered. *We were having a difficult time with ogres and trolls—great ugly devils they were, just people-looking enough to make them all the more repulsive. Used to jump us unexpectedly and kill all they could and then eat the corpses' brains. So we began to employ a barking code which, of course, they couldn't interpret. Perhaps in time it became the chief mode of speech. Yet you* speak *well enough.*

"I'm an unusual case," Dammy said. "I was picked out for special training."

I note the larynx has descended, as well as the lingual attachment, Sport said. *Makes barking easier, I suppose.*

"These ogres and trolls couldn't talk silently, I take it," Dammy said.

Quite right. A few barks and grunts—rather dull fellows.

"But it looks like they won," Dammy said. "Unless your boys are really our ancestors and not *erectus*. But I doubt it. You're not really Hominoidiae, I bet."

Curious idea, Sport said sadly. *Imagine people losing out to ogres and trolls! But you seem a human enough fellow, Dammy. So let's consider ourselves relatives in spite of all, even if only collaterally.* Again, Dammy shook all four hands.

How are things back home these days? Sport inquired genially. *Old dragons finally died out completely, did they? We used to see the odd one now and again—obviously only a few breeding pairs hanging on back in the hinterlands. Saw fewer every year. I remember the last one I saw.* (He graphically visualized what Dammy recognized as an iguanodon gumming foliage with toothless jaws.)

"We thought the last dinosaur cashed in his chips back in the Cretaceous," Dammy offered. "Based on the fossil record, of course."

Umm. It figures. Shy creatures. Always went off somewhere to die. We never found a dead one. Lots of stories about the Dragons' Graveyard, that sort of thing. I suppose they had a habit of heading for some spot of country that happened to be poor fossilizing ground. Knew one old fellow who claimed they swam out to sea. Trying to return to the old hatching ground, and continental drift had put an ocean between the dying dragon and his destination.

"Like lemmings," Dammy said. "Maybe so. It's as good an explanation as any. Consider the eels."

Sorry, they must be since my time—whatever it is you're referring to, that is. Eels are long skinny fish that we catch in the river. What about them?

"Both European and American eels breed in the part of the Atlantic known as the Sargasso Sea. Then they head for their home river—know instinctively which way to go. The theory is they started breeding in the Atlantic when it was just a long, skinny lake and kept on as it got wider. Sea turtles do the same sort of thing in the Pacific. Amazing, when you think of it—all those animals heading for geography that hasn't been there for a few million years."

Lots of changes, I suppose, Sport said. But the basics we can always count on: the Endless Forest, the inexhaustible supply of game, the rivers and lakes to give us plenty of good water and all the fish we can eat—all that can't change, no matter how tribal customs vary. I suppose I'd hear nothing but bark-

*ing if I went home now—but I could go off into the
forest depths and forget it.*

"The tribe made it big," Dammy said. "People
or ogres, or maybe a hybrid, but we spread out
until we came to the end of the Endless Forest and
met ourselves coming the other way."

So I suppose that Here is now a paradise indeed,
Sport hazarded. *No doubt we've mastered the big-
bitey things and the big-noisy things and the great-
big-shaggy things and so on, so that we can run
down the stripy-SOBs-that-run-like-the-devil in peace.*

"Maybe it figures," Dammy remarked. "Telepathy is the primitive form of communication;
birds and fish and insects seem to communicate
without barking, and although H. erectus had well-
developed Broca's and Wernicke's areas, and his
organized hunting suggests he could talk, his phar-
ynx and tongue weren't capable of true verbal
speech."

I'm enthralled, Sport said ecstatically. *Did we
ever solve the problems of drafty caves and crap
disposal? And lice and toothache and too-damn-cold
and too-damn-hot? Imagine! A world where we need
fear no animal . . .*

"Except man," Dammy said. "We settled down
to fighting among ourselves after we'd wiped out
the hyaenodons and the cave bears and the stab-
bing cats. And for the best of reasons. We *had* to,
to develop our character. The first hero was a man
with the guts to stand up to the reigning bully, not
the first man to stick a wooden spear in an enraged
bull mammouth."

We have much to discuss, Sport said. *Later, back
in the peace and coziness of my smooth place.*

"Like figuring out why we're hanging around

here waiting to find out what old Floss or Clace or Astrobe is going to cook up next?"

Astrobe is an interesting fellow, don't you think? Sport said while digging in his ear with a hind finger, after which he courteously offered to groom Dammy, who declined.

"It's some coincidence that we both come from Earth," Dammy said.

Not at all, was the reply. *You were placed here at my express request.*

"How did you know about me?"

I didn't—not personally. But being rather lonely at first, sometime ago I arranged, if any other of the people should happen along, that he be sent to me.

"How did you get here?" Dammy asked.

It was rather odd. I was gathering long-yellow-sweet food, when a big-bitey thing appeared quite suddenly, directly in my path, a rather narrow cleft in the rock. I turned to flee and saw a strange Person; a moment later I awakened in a place-that-was-smooth, the first of many I was to see.

"Snatched just like me," Dammy commented. "And what have you been doing since?"

Eating and eliminating, mostly, plus sleeping. From time to time the ancestral-spirits-that-can't-get-into-the-underworld come along and take me outside for a bit of fun here in the arena. Last time it was hungry dire-beast; rather a bore, actually. It's so simple to distract the poor things into eating the fellows who run the show.

"Pitted against wild animals in the arena," Dammy mused. "And you call that fun. How often does it happen?"

Quite frequently. About once each five thousand years, I should imagine.

"Just for a second there I started to worry," Dammy said lazily. "I guess I'll take a nap. How long has it been since the last time?"

Try the pavement. Sport suggested. *About five thousand years, give or take the odd decade.*

"Oh. Then I guess I can relax." Dammy stretched out on the resilient, body-temperature surface.

How I admire your aplomb, Sport commented. *I rather doubt that I would be capable of dozing off under the circumstances.*

"What circumstances?" Dammy inquired vaguely. "You told me it's no sweat. So why not grab some shut-eye?"

The circumstances, a chilly mind-voice cut in, *that you are guilty of high crimes against the state and are unlikely to receive a recommendation for clemency.*

"Wait a minute!" Dammy blurted, sitting up. "I got a right to a mouthpiece!" He got to his feet. "And anyway, you'll have to catch me first."

Reaching deep into his inner resources—an unexpectedly shallow repository after all, Dammy noted—he levitated, floating in a vertical position just clear of the arena floor for a few moments; then he rotated to a face-down, horizontal orientation and at once shot upward so rapidly that the arena below seemed to dwindle in an instant to postage-stamp size before Dammy lost it in the intricacy of the vast city spreading below him. Far away, hazy gray-green hills formed the horizon. Without conscious effort, he darted this way and that, delighted with the sensation of flying high. He was aware of a distant buzzing and then saw a swarm of gnats in the distance, a swarm that churned aimlessly for a moment before resolving itself into a stream aimed more or less in his direction. As the leading gnat grew closer, Dammy realized with surprise that it was very large for an insect—that it was, in fact, about the size of an F-115, and similarly ferocious in appearance. Its shock wave *boom!*ed and then it was past, only a shower of stinging pellets impinging on Dammy's exposed awareness indicating its hostile intention. Dammy easily shunted aside the projectiles, hundred-millimeter high-explosive anti-aircraft cannon shells, he noted in passing. They exploded harmlessly immediately after ricocheting from his hastily erected defensive aura. The second, and then three craft abreast, fired equally futile bursts at him. A heavier weapon-system now approached, angled up to shoot above him, dropping a small nuclear bomb that arched sharply toward him.

Wait a minute! Dammy thought frantically. *I can't handle the heavy stuff! No fair! Help!*

"I dislike to intrude," Sport's soft, audible voice spoke up. "But may I be of assistance?"

Confusedly Dammy twisted to catch a glimpse of his pal's shaggy, long-limbed form in a reclining pose, floating as easily as he, himself, it seemed. "Welcome to our group," Dammy said. "But it looks like our group is about to be dispersed." He *reached*, touched the armed and down-counting bomb, now only 3.08 meters distant and falling at a rate of 300 meters per second, allowing him a full one-hundredth of a second in which to act. He *thrust*, feeling the last of his strength draining away, and was aware of a vast relief as the nuke went spinning off to disappear as suddenly as the attack squadron that had launched it.

"Let's get out of here," Dammy suggested, suddenly vividly aware of his exposed position, hanging unsupported, in full view, 2,406 meters, three centimeters above the capital city.

Sport was sitting across the table from him, his usually merry expression somewhat glum in the yellow glow of the sputtering candle. He refilled their smeared jelly glasses from a nearly empty hand-blown bottle. Dammy grabbed his and took it at a gulp. It was reject grade mimblefruit brandy from Osvo 3, cut 50–50 with straight wood alcohol, he noticed, uncaring.

"Sport!" he exclaimed. "How? What? . . . and all the other interrogatives too," he choked, then continued silently.

I had the damnedest dream. I was flying, and things got kind of hairy, and you were with me—and here we are.

So we are, Sport agreed silently. *You are an adventurous fellow, Dammy,* he commented reproachfully. *Curious that you always manage to do the unexpected. But why did you send me that urgent message to meet you here, in this deserted subvault?*

"I didn't," Dammy managed to say aloud, wondering if his vocal apparatus were permanently damaged.

But it seemed to be quite unmistakably your voice, Sport insisted. *It was just after you'd made that remark about needing something called a "pack of butts" and went into the male eliminatorium. I waited, but you didn't return, so I started to go in myself to see if all was well. Then I got the message, with its precise directions as to how to get here.* Sport paused to shudder.

"I have perfect confidence in your wisdom, of

course, Dammy, but I don't quite see how we're to get out again, having welded the lock mechanisms to discourage pursuit." Sport was speaking aloud again, Dammy noticed. Possibly he felt that, after all, his hairless friend understood barking better.

"We were in the arena," Dammy said carefully, attempting to orient himself.

"Yes, I recall it well," Sport replied. "Only two hundred of your years ago, yet it's as fresh as if it were yesterday."

"It hasn't been half an hour," Dammy said desperately.

Sport looked distressed. To his surprise, Dammy felt the delicate mind-touch of his friend, probing without prior permission, a thing he had never done before.

"Oh, dear," Sport said unhappily. "This is dreadful! How could they? Or—how did they? My fault entirely; I had simply assumed too much. But there it is—no help for it now, I fear. It's up to you alone, Dammy. I'd help if I could, but you understand better than I—"

"Do I?" Dammy inquired, frowning. "What's the beef, Sport? Did I do something wrong?"

"Not wrong in any moral sense, Dammy, but tactically, perhaps. Still, I suppose it was the only way to recoup the earlier blunder."

"Tell me straight out, Sport," Dammy appealed. "What's wrong?"

Sport looked at him solemnly with large, brown monkey eyes. "You died, Dammy old fellow. I'm sorry, but there it is. You're dead."

"That was careless of me," Dammy agreed. "But I never thought it would be like this: no angels, no harps—but no little fellows with tails and horns and pitchforks, either. Maybe I better quit while I'm ahead."

"Are you willing to do so, Dammy?" Sport asked urgently.

"Sure," Dammy said emphatically. "Who wants to be a corpse?"

"Try to remember," Sport suggested. "You recall that long-ago time in the arena at Trisme? Good. Hold on to that."

"Nothing to it," Dammy said. "But after that . . ."

"Never mind that," Sport advised solemnly. "I don't quite understand what's happening here, but I feel sure your profound recollection of the arena affair is significant. So cling to that. Regard the rest as a dream. Try, Dammy. Perhaps you can do it. You've gone too far for outside help to reach you. Try.

Dammy tried . . .

Oh, dear. Sport's gentle mind-voice penetrated Dammy's restless dream. *Here it is. . . . Oh, big-horny-devils, just as I'd hoped: one longs for a challenge.*

"Two will settle for bunny wabbit," Dammy commented, and blinked against the harsh sunlight. From the same dark entry from which Sport had emerged a few minutes earlier, something vast and noisy thundered, snorting with effort. Sport dropped to all fours and galloped forward as if to intercept the immense creature.

The beast he was advancing to meet was no larger, Dammy estimated, than a TD-18' dozer, and about as dainty. It was massive in build, with four legs, and a flaring shield of armor behind the three-horned head. Dammy felt the ground tremble under its charge. It was, he realized, an adult Triceratops, alive and healthy, though apparently in a bad mood. Sport altered course to cut across in front of the monster, which ignored him to continue its blind charge. Sport halted, rose to his rear limbs, waved cheerfully to Dammy, and ran two-legged after the retreating dinosaur, which had slowed to a trot. Sport came up alongside, matched pace, reached for a grip on the nearest horn, and lightly leaped astride. The ornithischian seemed not to notice. The crowd muttered.

I'll have to stir him up a bit—Sport's comment came clearly to Dammy—*or they'll shoot this poor gentle old fellow and bring in something uglier.*

Don't go to any trouble on my account, Dammy replied.

Foreword to an excerpt from
The Other Side of Time

One of the things I had not anticipated when I began my exploration of the multiordinate manifold of universes which constitute reality, was the intricacy of the interrelationships both linking and separating the parallel worlds. When the difference of a millimeter in the position of a single grain of sand is sufficient to define a distinct world-line, developing in isolation from all the others which lie so close at hand and yet at such vast distances, it is clear that many phenomena will remain indistinguishably the same, out to many parameters from the Common History Line, and persons and events that are perfectly (or almost) familiar will appear in close conjunction with the most outré variations imaginable. I think we exist simultaneously in a wide swath of very closely related lines: (after all, that grain of sand isn't likely to have affected our individual heritages and development enough to show) thus, we find curious little discrepancies from time to time, like the document we know we put in the 'Contracts' file, but which isn't there—and is never seen again.

An excerpt from
The Other Side of Time

It was three days before I felt strong enough to pay my call on Mother Goodwill. Her cottage was a thatch-roofed rectangle of weathered stone almost lost under a tangle of wrist-sized rose vines heavy with deep red blossoms. I squeezed through a rusted gate, picked my way along a path overhung with untrimmed rhododendron, lifted the huge brass knocker and clanked it against the low black oak door. Through the one small, many-paned window, I caught a glimpse of the corner table, a pot of forget-me-nots, a thick leatherbound book. There was a humming of bees in the air, a scent of flowers, and a whiff of fresh-brewed coffee. Not the traditional setting for calling on a witch, I thought. . . .

The door opened. Mother Goodwill, looking neat in a white shirt and peasant skirt, favored me with a sad smile, motioning me in.

"No Halloween costume today," I commented.

"You're feeling better, Mr. Bayard," she said drily. "Will you have a mug of coffee? Or is't not customary in your native land?"

I shot her a sharp look. "Skeptical already?"

Her shoulders lifted and dropped. "I believe what my senses tell me. Sometimes they seem to contra-

dict each other." I took a chair at the table, glanced
around the small room. It was scrupulously clean
and tidy, furnished with the kind of rustic authen-
ticity that would have had the ladies of the DAR
back home oohing and aahing and overworking
the word "quaint." Mother Goodwill brought the
pot over, poured two cups, put cream and sugar
on the table, then sat.

"Well, Mr. Bayard, is your mind clear this
morning, your remembrance well restored?"

I nodded, tried the coffee. It was good.

"Don't you have some other name I could call
you?" I asked. "Mother Goodwill goes with the
fright wig and the warts."

"You may call me Olivia." She had slim, white
hands, and on one finger a fine green stone twinkled.
She sipped her coffee and looked at me, as though
making up her mind to tell me something.

"You were going to ask me questions," I prompted
her. "After I've answered them, maybe you'll clear
up a few matters for me."

"Many were the wonders you babbled of in your
delirium," she said. I heard a tiny clatter, glanced
at her cup; a fine tremor was rattling it against
the saucer. She put it down quickly, ducked her
hands out of sight.

"Oft have I sensed that there was more to existence than this . . ." she waved a hand to take in
everything. "In dreams I've glimpsed enchanted
hills and my heart yearned out to them, and I'd
wake with the pain of something beautiful and
lost that haunted me long after. I think in your
wild talk, there was that which made a certain
hope spring up again—a hope long forgotten, with
the other hopes of youth. Now tell me, stranger,

that talk of other worlds, like each to other as new-struck silver pieces, yet each with a tiny difference, and of a strange coach, with the power to fly from one to the next—all this was fancy, eh? The raving of a mind sore vexed with meddling—"

"It's true—Olivia," I cut in. "I know it's hard to grasp at first. I seem to recall I was a bit difficult to convince, once. We're accustomed to thinking we know everything. There's a powerful tendency to disbelieve anything that doesn't fit the pre-conception."

"You spoke of trouble, Brion . . ." she spoke my name easily, familiarly. I suppose sharing someone's innermost thoughts tends to relax formalities. I didn't mind. Olivia without her disguise was a charming woman, in spite of her severe hairdo and prison pallor. With a little sunshine and just a touch of makeup—

I pulled myself back to the subject at hand.

She listened attentively as I told her the whole story, from Richthofen's strange interrogation to my sentencing by the Xonijeelians.

"So I'm stuck," I finished. "Without a shuttle, I'm trapped here for the rest of my days."

She shook her head. "These are strange things, Brion, things I should not believe, so wild and fantastic are they. And yet—I do believe. . . ."

"From what little I've learned of this world line, it's backward technologically—"

"Why, we're a very modern people," Olivia said. "We have steam power—the ships on the Atlantic run make the crossing in nine days—and there are the balloons, the telegraph, and telephone, our modern coal-burning road cars, which are beginning to replace the horse in many parts of the colonies, even—"

"Sure, I know, Olivia—no offense intended. Let's just say that in some areas we're ahead of you. The Imperium has the M-C drive. My own native world has nuclear power, jet aircraft, radar, and a primitive space program. Here you've gone in other directions. The point is, I'm stranded here. They've exiled me to a continuum I can never escape from."

"Is it so ill then, Brion? You have a whole world here before you—and now that the artificial barriers have been cleansed from your mind, you'll freely recall these wonders you left behind!" She was speaking eagerly now, excited at the prospect. "You spoke of aircraft. Build one! How marvelous to fly in the sky like a bird! Your coming here could mean the dawn of a new Age of Glory for the Empire!"

"Uh-huh," I said ungraciously. "That's great. But what about *my* world? By now the Hagroon have probably launched their attack—and maybe succeeded with it! My wife may be wearing chains now instead of pearls!" I got up, stamped over to the window and stared out. "While I rot here, in this backwater world," I snarled.

"Brion," she said softly behind me. "You find yourself troubled—not so much by the threat to your beloved friends as by the quality of remoteness these matters have taken on. . . ."

I turned. "What do you mean, remote? Barbro, my friends, in the hands of these ape-men—"

"Those who tampered with your mind, Brion, sought to erase these things from your memory. True, my skill availed to lift the curse, but 'tis no wonder that they seem to you now as old memories, a tale told long ago. And I myself gave a command to you while yet you slept, that the pain of loss be eased—"

"The pain of loss be damned! If I hadn't been fool enough to trust Dzok—"

"Poor Brion. Know you not yet it was he who gulled you while you slept, planted the desire to go with him to Xonijeel? Yet he did his best for you—or so your memory tells."

"I could have taken the shuttle back," I said flatly. "At least I'd have been there, to help fight the bastards off."

"And yet, the wise ones, the monkey-men of Xonijeel, told you that this Zero-zero world did not exist—"

"They're crazy!" I took a turn up and down the room. "There's too much here I don't understand, Olivia! I'm like a man wandering in the dark, banging into things he can't quite get his hands on. And now—" I raised my hands and let them fall, suddenly inexpressibly weary.

"You have your life still ahead, Brion. You will make a new place for yourself here. Accept that which cannot be changed."

I came back and sat down.

"Olivia, I haven't asked Gunvor and the others many questions. I didn't want to arouse curiosity by my ignorance. The indoctrination Dzok and his boys gave me didn't cover much—just enough to get me started. I suppose they figured I'd get to a library and brief myself. Tell me something about this world. Fill me in on your history, to start with."

She laughed—an unexpectedly merry sound.

"How charming, Brion, to be called upon to

describe this humdrum old world as though it were a dreamer's fancy—a might-have-been, instead of dull reality."

I managed a sour smile. "Reality's always a little dull to whoever's involved in it."

"Where shall I begin? With Ancient Rome? The Middle Ages?"

"The first thing to do is establish a Common History date—the point at which your world diverged from mine. You mentioned 'The Empire.' What empire? When was it founded?"

"Why the Empire of France, of course." Olivia blinked, then shook her head. "But then, nothing is 'of course'," she said. "I speak of the Empire established by Bonaparte, in 1799."

"So far so good," I said. "We had a Bonaparte, too. But his empire didn't last long. He abdicated and was sent off to Elba in 1814."

"Yes, but he escaped, returned to France, and led his armies to glorious victory!"

I was shaking my head. "He was free for a thousand days, until the British defeated him at Waterloo. He was sent to St. Helena and died a few years later."

Olivia stared at me. "How strange—how eerie, and how strange. The Emperor Napoleon ruled in splendor at Paris for twenty-three years after his great victory at Brussels, and died in 1837 at Nice. He was succeeded by his son, Louis—"

"The Duke of Reichstadt?"

"No. The Duke died in his youth, of consumption. Louis was a boy of sixteen, the son of the Emperor and the Princess of Denmark."

"And his Empire still exists," I mused.

"After the abdication of the English tyrant,

George, the British Isles were permitted to enter the Empire as a special ward of the Emperor. After the unification of Europe, enlightenment was brought to the Asians and Africans. Today, they are semiautonomous provinces, administered from Paris, but with their own local Houses of Deputies empowered to deal with internal matters. As for New France—or Louisiana—this talk of rebellion will soon die down. A royal commission has been sent to look into the complaints against the Viceroy."

"I think we've got the C. H. date pretty well pinned down," I said. "Eighteen-fourteen. And it looks as though there's been no significant scientific or technological progress since."

This prompted questions which I answered at length. Olivia was an intelligent and well-educated woman. She was enthralled by my picture of a world without the giant shadow of Bonaparte falling across it.

The morning had developed into the drowsy warmth of noon by the time I finished. Olivia offered me lunch and I accepted. While she busied herself at the wood-burning stove, I sat by the window, sipping a stone mug of brown beer, looking out at this curious, anachronistic landscape of tilled fields, a black-topped road along which a horse pulled a rubber-tired carriage, the white and red dots of farmhouses across the valley. There was an air of peace and plenty that made my oddly distant recollection of the threat to the Imperium seem, as Olivia said, like a half-forgotten story, read long ago—like something in the book lying on the table. I picked up the fat, red leather-bound volume, glanced at the title:

The Sorceress of Oz, by Lyman F. Baum.

"That's funny," I said.

Olivia glanced over at the book in my hands, smiled almost shyly.

"Strange reading matter for a witch, you think? But on these fancies my own dreams sometimes love to dwell, Brion. As I told you, this one narrow world seems not enough."

"It's not that, Olivia. We've pretty well established that our C. H. date is early in the nineteenth century. Baum wasn't born until about 1855 or so—nearly half a century later. But here he is."

I flipped the book open, noted the publisher— Wiley & Cotton, New York, New Orleans, and Paris—and the date: 1896.

"You know this book, in your own strange world?" Olivia asked.

I shook my head. "In my world he never wrote this one." I was admiring the frontispiece by W. W. Denslow, showing a Glinda-like figure facing a group of gnomes. The next page had an elaborate initial "I" at the top, followed by the words: " '. . . summoned you here,' said Sorana the Sorceress, 'to tell you . . .' "

"It was my favorite book as a child," Olivia said. "But if you know it not, how then do you recognize the author's name?"

"He wrote others. *The Wizard of Oz* was the first book I ever read all the way through."

"The Wizard of Oz? Not the Sorceress? How enchanting it would be to read it!"

"Is this the only one he wrote?"

"Sadly, yes. He died the following year—1897."

"Eighteen ninety-seven; that could mean . . ." I trailed off. The fog that had been hanging over my mind for days since I had awakened here was rapidly dissipating in the brisk wind of a sudden realization: Dzok and his friends had relocated me, complete with phony memories to replace the ones they'd tried to erase, in a world-line as close as possible to my own. They'd been clever, thorough, and humane. But not quite as clever as they thought, a bit less thorough in their research than they should have been—and altogether too humane.

I remembered the photogram the councillors had shown me—and the glowing point, unknown to Imperial Net cartographers, which represented a fourth, undiscovered world lying within the Blight. I had thought at the time that it was an error, along with the other, greater error that had omitted the Zero-zero line of the Imperium.

But it had been no mistake. B-I Four existed—a world with a Common History date far more recent than the 15th century, the C.H. date of the closest lines beyond the Blight.

And I was there—or here—in a world where, in 1897, at least one man known in my own world had existed. And if one, why not another—or two others: Maxoni and Cocini, inventors of the M-C drive.

"Could mean what, Brion?" Olivia's voice jarred me back to the present.

"Nothing. Just a thought." I put the book down. "I suppose it's only natural that even fifty years after a major divergence, not everything would have been affected. Some of the same people would be born."

"Brion," Olivia looked at me across the room. "I won't ask you to trust me, but let me help you."

"Help me with what?" I tried to recapture the casual expression I'd been wearing up until a moment before, but I could feel it freezing on my face like a mud pack.

"You have made a plan; I sense it. Alone, you cannot succeed. There is too much that is strange to you here, too many pitfalls to betray you. Let me lend you what help I can."

"Why should you want to help me—if I were planning something?"

She looked at me for a minute without answering, her dark eyes wide in her pale, classic face.

"I've spent my life in search for a key to some other world ... some dreamworld of my mind. Somehow, you seem to be a link, Brion. Even if I can never go there, it would please me to know I'd helped someone to reach the unattainable shore."

"They're all worlds, just like this one, Olivia. Some better, some worse—some much worse. They're all made up of people and earth and buildings, the same old natural laws, the same old human nature. You can't find your dreamworld by packing up and moving on; you've got to build it where you are."

"And yet, I see the ignorance, the corruption, the social and moral decay, the lies, the cheating, the treachery of those who hold the trust of the innocent—"

"Sure, and until we've evolved a human society to match our human intelligence, those things will exist. But give us time, Olivia—we've only been experimenting with culture for a few thousand years. A few thousand more will make a lot of difference."

She laughed. "You speak as though an age were but a moment."

"Compared with the time it took us to evolve from an amoeba to an ape—or even from the first *Homo sapiens* to the first tilled field—it *is* a moment. But don't give up your dreams. They're the force that carries us on toward whatever our ultimate goal is."

"Then let me lend that dream concrete reality. Let me help you, Brion. The story they told me—that you had fallen ill from overwork as an official of the Colonial Office, that you were here for a rest cure—'tis as thin as a Parisian nightdress! And, Brion . . ." She lowered her voice. "You are watched."

"Watched? By whom—a little man with a beard and dark glasses?"

" 'Tis no jest, Brion! I saw a man last night lurking by the gate at Gunvor's house—and half an hour since, a man well muffled up in scarves passed in the road yonder, as you sipped coffee."

"That doesn't prove anything."

She shook her head impatiently. "You plan to fly, I know that. I know also that your visit to me will arouse the curiosity of those who prison you here."

"Prison me? Why, I'm as free as a bird—"

"You waste time, Brion," she cut me off. "What deed you committed, or why, I know not; but in a contest between you and drab officialdom, I'll support your cause. Now, quickly, Brion! Where will you go? How will you travel? What plan will—"

"Hold on, Olivia! You're jumping to conclusions!"

"And jump you must, if you'd evade the hounds

of the hunter! I sense danger closing about you as a snare about the roebuck's neck!"

"I've told you, Olivia. I was exiled here by the Xonijeelian Council. They didn't believe my story— or pretended not to. They dumped me here to be rid of me—they fancy themselves as humane, you know. If they'd meant to kill me, they had every opportunity to do so."

"They sought to mesmerize your knowledge of the past away; now they watch, their results to judge. And when they see you restive, familiar of a witch—"

"You're no witch—"

"As such all know me here. 'Twas an ill gambit that brought you here by daylight, Brion."

"If I'd crept out at midnight, they'd have seen me anyway—if they're watching me as you seem to think—and they'd have known damned well I wasn't satisfied with their hand-painted picture of my past."

"In any case, they'll like it not. They'll come again, take you away, and once again essay to numb your knowledge of the worlds, and of your past."

I thought that over. "They might, at that," I said. "I don't suppose it was part of their relocation program to have me spreading technical knowledge among the primitives."

"Where will you go, Brion?"

I hesitated; but what the hell, Olivia was right. I had to have help. And if she intended to betray me, she had plenty on me already.

"Rome," I said.

She nodded. "Very well. What is the state of your purse?"

"I have a bank account—"

"Leave that. Luckily, I have my store of gold Napoleons buried in the garden."

"I don't want your money."

"Nonsense. We'll both need it. I'm going with you."

"You can't—"

"Can, and will!" she said, her dark eyes alight. "Make ready, Brion! We leave this very night!"

"This is crazy," I whispered to the dark, hooded figure standing beside me on the shadowed path. "There's no reason for you to get involved in this."

"Hush," Olivia said softly. "Now he grows restless. See him there? I think he'll cross the road now, more closely to spy us out."

I watched the dense shadows, made out the figure of a man. He moved off, crossed the road a hundred yards below the cottage, disappeared among the trees on our side. I shifted my weight carefully, itching under the wild getup Olivia had assembled for me—warty face, gnarly hands, stringy white hair, and all. I looked like Mother Goodwill's older brother—as ill-tempered an old duffer as ever gnashed his gums at the carryings-on of the younger generation. Olivia was done up like Belle Watling in three layers of paint, a fancy red wig, a purple dress that fit her trim figure like wet silk, and enough bangles, rings, beads, and tinkly earrings to stock a gyfte shoppe.

"Hist—he steals closer now," my coconspirator whispered. "Another half minute."

I waited, listening to the monotonous chirrup of crickets in a nearby field, the faraway *oo-mau* of a cow, the yapping of a farm dog. After dark, the world belonged to the animals.

Olivia's hand touched mine. "Now." I followed as she stepped silently off. I had to crouch slightly to keep below the level of the ragged hedge. There was no moon, only a little faint starlight to help us pick a way along the rutted dirt road. We reached the end of the hedge, and I motioned Olivia back, stole a look toward the house. A head was clearly silhouetted against the faint light from the small side window.

"It's okay," I said in a low voice. "He's at the window."

There was a crunch of gravel, and a light snapped on, played across the ruts, flashed over me, settled on Olivia.

"Here, woman," a deep voice growled. "What're ye doing abroad after bell-toll?"

Olivia planted a hand on her hip, tossed her head, not neglecting to smile archly.

"Aoow, Capting," she purred. "Ye fair give me a turn! It's only me old gaffer, what oi'm seein' orf to the rile-trine."

"Gaffer, is it?" The light dwelt on me again briefly, went back to caress Olivia's sequined bosom. "Haven't seen ye about the village before. Where ye from?"

"I float about, as ye might say, Major. A tourist, like ye might call me."

"On shank's mare, in the middle of the night? Queer idea o' fun, I call it—and with yer gaffer, too. Better let me see yer identity papers, ducks."

"Well, as it 'appens, I come away in such a rush, they seem to 'ave got left behind."

"Like that, is't?" I heard a snort from the unseen

man behind the light—one of the roving security police who were a fixture of this world, I guessed. "Run off with a fistful o' spoons, did ye? Or maybe lifted one purse too many—"

"Nofink o' that sort! What cheek! I'm an honest, licensed tart, plying 'er profession and keeping her old gaffer, what oi'm the sole support of!"

"Never mind, love. I won't take ye in. A wee sample of yer wares, and I'll forget I ever saw ye." He came close, and a big hand reached out toward Olivia. She let out a sharp squeak and jumped back. The cop brushed past me. I caught a glimpse of a tricorn hat, a beak nose, loose jowls, a splash of color on the collar of the uniform. I picked my spot, chopped down hard across the base of his neck with the side of my hand. He yelped, dropped the light, stumbled to hands and knees. The stiff collar had protected him from the full force of the blow. He scrambled, trying to rise; I followed, kicked him square under the chin. He back-flipped and sprawled out, unconscious. I grabbed up the light and found the switch, flicked it off.

"Is he . . . badly hurt?" Olivia was staring at the smear of blood at the corner of the slack mouth.

"He'll have trouble asking for bribes for a few weeks." I pulled Olivia back toward the hedgerow. "Let's hope our snooper didn't hear anything."

We waited for a minute, then started off again, hurrying now. Far away, a spark of wavering, yellowish light moved across the slope of the hill beyond the village.

"That's the train," Olivia said. "We'll have to hurry!"

We walked briskly for 15 minutes, passed the darkened shops at the edge of town, reached the station just as the puffing coal-burner pulled in. A severe-looking clerk in a dark uniform with crossed chest straps and coattails accepted Olivia's money, wrote out tickets by hand, pointed out our car. Inside we found wide seats upholstered in green plush. We were the only passengers. I leaned back in my seat with a sigh. The train whistle shrilled, and a lurch ran through the car.

"We're on our way," Olivia breathed. She looked ecstatic, like a kid at the fair.

"We're just going to Rome," I said. "Not the land of Oz."

"Who can say whither the road of the future leads?"

At the Albergo Romulus, Olivia and I had adjoining rooms well up under the eaves, with ceilings that slanted down to a pair of dormer windows opening onto a marketplace with a handsome Renaissance fountain, the incessant flutter of pigeons' wings, and a day and night shrilling of excited Italian voices. We were sitting at the small table in my room, eating a late breakfast of pizzas, washed down with a musty red wine that cost so little that even the local begging corps could afford to keep a mild buzz on most of the time.

"The two men I'm interested in were born somewhere in northern Italy about 1850," I told Olivia. "They came to Rome as young men, studied engineering and electronics, and in 1893 made the basic discovery that gave the Imperium the Net drive. I'm gambling that if Baum managed to get himself born, and in the Nineties was writing something pretty close to what he did in my world—and in the Zero-zero A-line too—then maybe Maxoni and Cocini existed here too. They didn't perfect the M-C drive, obviously—or if they did, the secret died with them—but maybe they came close. Maybe they left something I can use."

"Brion, did you not tell me that all the worlds that lie about your Zero-zero line are desolate, blasted into ruin by these very forces? Is it safe to tamper with such fell instruments as these?"

"I'm a fair shuttle technician, Olivia. I know most of the danger points. Maxoni and Cocini didn't realize what they were playing with. They stumbled on the field by blind luck."

"And in a thousand million other worlds of might-have-been they failed, and brought ruin in their wake. . . ."

"You knew all this when we left Harrow," I said shortly. "It's my only chance—and a damned poor chance it is, I'll admit. But I can't build a shuttle from scratch—there's a specially wound coil that's the heart of the field-generator. I've installed 'em, but I never tried to wind one. Maybe—if there was a Maxoni here, and a Cocini—and they made the same chance discovery, wrote up their notes like good little researchers, the notes still exist, and I can find them—"

Olivia laughed—a charming, girlish laugh. "If the gods decree that all those *ifs* are in your favor—why then 'tis plain, they mean you to press on. I'll risk it, Brion. The vision of the Sapphire City still beckons me."

"It's the Emerald City, where I come from," I said. "But we won't quibble over details. Let's see if we can find those notes first. We'll have plenty of time then to decide what to do with them."

An hour later, at the local equivalent of a municipal record center, a tired-looking youth in a narrow-cut black suit showed me a three-foot ledger in which names were written in spidery longhand—thousands of names, followed by dates, places of birth, addresses, and other pertinent details.

"Sicuro, Signore," he said in a tone of weary superiority, "the municipality, having nothing to hide, throws open to you its records—among the most complete archives in existence in the Empire—but as for reading them . . ." he smirked, tweaked his hairline mustache. "That the Signore must do for himself."

"Just explain to me what I'm looking at," I suggested gently. "I'm looking for a record of Giulio Maxoni, or Carlo Cocini—"

"Yes, yes, so you said. And here before you is the registration book in which the names of all new arrivals in the city were recorded at the time identity papers were issued. They came to Rome in 1870, you said—or was it 1880? You seemed uncertain. As for me . . ." he spread his hands. "I am even more uncertain. I have never heard of these relatives, or friends, or ancestors—or whatever they might be. In them, you, it appears, have an interest. As for me—I have none. There is the book, covering the decade in question. Look all you wish. But do not demand miracles of me! I have duties to perform!" His voice developed an irritated snap on the last words. He strutted off to sulk somewhere back in the stacks. I grunted and started looking.

Twenty minutes passed quietly. We worked our way through 1870, started on 1871. The busy archivist peered out once to see what we were doing, withdrew after a sour look. Olivia and I stood at the wooden counter, poring over the crabbed longhand, each taking one page of about two hundred names. She was a fast reader; before I had finished my page, she had turned to the next. Half a minute later she gave a sharp gasp.

"Brion! Look! Guilio Maxoni, born 1847 at Paglio; trade, artificer—"

I looked. It was the right name. I tried not to let myself get too excited, but my pulse picked up in spite of the voice of prudence whispering in my ear that there might be hundreds of Giulio Maxonis.

"Nice work, girl," I said in a cool, controlled voice that only broke twice on the three words. "What address?"

She read it off. I jotted it down in a notebook I had thoughtfully provided for the purpose, added the other data from the ledger. We searched for another hour, but found no record of Cocini. The clerk came back and hovered, as though we'd overstayed our welcome. I closed the book and shoved it across the counter to him.

"Don't sweat it, Jack," I said genially. "We're just making up a sucker list for mailings on budget funerals."

"Mailings?" He stared at me suspiciously. "Municipal records are not intended for such uses—and in any event, these people are all long since dead!"

"Exactly," I agreed. "A vast untapped market for our line of goods. Thanks heaps. I'll make a note to give you special treatment when your time comes."

We walked away in a silence you could have cut into slabs with a butter knife.

Foreword to an excerpt from
Earthblood

In the year of grace 1962, I was on active duty in the USAF, stationed at HQ, 3AF, near London. One evening I had a phone call from a sprightly feminine voice which identified itself as Rosel Jawj Brown. At once that unfathomable mystery called memory produced a datum, and I said, "Whose work has appeared in The Magazine of Fantasy and Science Fiction?"*

The connection was established. Rosel was in London for a year with her husband, Professor Brown of Tulane, on some sort of scholarly exchange program. I suggested they visit us, they did, and Rosel and I discussed writing a novel in collaboration. She was cool to the idea, since she had had a bad experience attempting a collaboration on a dense novel set in medieval Germany, an effort proposed by a Name writer who shall be nameless just this once. He was to supply all the authentic background, and Rosel was to attend to the trifling chore of actually writing the book. After she had produced a vast pile of manuscript, dutifully putting in all of his arcane lore, he baldly suggested one day that she was merely trying to capitalize on his Big Name. Rosel, not noted for suffering fools gladly, quietly placed the nearly complete manuscript in the fireplace, where a cheery blaze was blazing cheerily. The Big Name tried to salvage it, but, alas, it went on to brennschluss. Thus she wasn't keen to try again. A few days later, the first line of our collaborative novel appeared in my mental field of vision, complete and perfect. I at once phoned Rosel and told her, and she at once corrected me and told me how it should go. The collaboration was off and running!

The way in which humanity is distinguished from the commonality of intelligent species in our Galaxy is not in his urbanity, subtlety, and sophistication, but in his raw animal vigor. While the other star-traveling races all have written histories covering millions of years, we are only a few tens of thousands of years from our cave-dwelling forebears, and old Grandpa, slumbering in our deep brain, once awakened, still has all his old stuff.

An excerpt from
Earthblood

The surgeon licked his lipless mandibles, peeling off the protective film under which the burns on Roan's shoulder and arm had been healing for many weeks.

"Eh, pretty, very pretty! Pink and new as a fresh-hatched suckling! There'll be no scars to mar that smooth hide!"

"Ouch!" Roan said. "That hurts."

"Ignore it, youngling," the surgeon said absently, working Roan's elbow joint. He nodded to himself, tried the wrist and then the fingers.

"All limber enough; now raise your limb here." He indicated shoulder level. Roan lifted his arm, wincing. The surgeon's horny fingers went to the shoulder joint, prodding and kneading.

"No loss of tone there," the surgeon muttered. "Bend over, stretch your back."

Roan bent, twisted, working the shoulder, stretching the newly healed burns. Sweat popped out on his forehead.

"At first it may feel as though the skin is tearing open," the surgeon said. "But it's nothing."

Roan straightened. "I'll try to remember that."

The surgeon was nodding, closing his instrument case. "You'll soon regain full use of the limb. Meanwhile, the hide is tender, and there'll be a certain stiffness in the joints."

"Can I—ah—do heavy work now?"

"In moderation. But take care: I've no wish to see my prize exhibit damaged." The surgeon rubbed his hard hands together with a chirruping sound. "Wait until Henry Dread sees this," he cackled. "Calls me a Geek, does he? Threatens to put me out the air lock, eh? But where would he ever find another surgeon of my skill?" He darted a final, sharp glance of approval at Roan and was gone. Roan pulled his tunic over his head, buckled his belt in place, and stretched his arms gingerly. There was a wide header over the doorway. He went to

it, grasped it, and pulled himself up carefully. The
sensation reminded him of a Charon he had seen
stripping hide from a dead gracyl ... but the in-
jured arm held his weight.

He dropped back and went out into the corridor.
There was a broken packing case in a reclamation
bin in the corner. Roan wrenched a three-foot length
of tough, blackish inch-thick wood from it. He
looked toward the bright-lit intersection of the main
concourse. A steward in soiled whites waddled past
on bowed legs, holding a tray up on a stumpy arm.
Henry Dread and his officers would be drinking in
the wardroom now. It was as good a time as any ...

Roan turned and followed the dull red indicator
lights toward the lower decks.

He was in a narrow corridor ill lit by grimed-
over glare panels. Voices yammered nearby: shouts,
snarls, a drunken song, a bellow of anger; the
third watch break hour was underway in the crew
quarters. Roan hefted the skrilwood club. It was
satisfactorily heavy.

Feet clumped in the cross-corridor 10 feet away.
Roan ducked into a side passage, flattened himself,
watched two round-backed barrel-chested human-
oids high-step past on unshod three-toed feet, bells
tied to their leg lacings jingling at each step. When
they had passed, he emerged, following the tiny
green numbers that glowed over doors, found one
larger than the others. Roan listened at the door;
there was a dull mumble of voices. He slid the
panel aside, stepped in; it was a barracks, and he
wrinkled his nose at the thick fudgy odor of un-
washed bedding, alien bodies, spilled wine, decay.
A narrow, littered passage led between bunks. A

dull-eyed Chronid looked up at him from an un-kempt bed. Roan went past, stepping over scattered boots, empty bottles, a pair of six-toed feet in tattered socks sprawling from a rump-sprung canvas chair. Halfway along the room, four large Minids crouched on facing benches, bald heads together. They looked up. One of them was Snaggle-head.

He gaped; then his wide lips stretched in a cold grin. He thrust aside a leather wine mug, wiped his mouth with the back of a thick, square hand, and got to his feet. He reached behind his back, brought out a knife with an 18-inch blade, whetted it across his bare forearm.

"Well, looky what's got loose from its string—" he started.

"Don't talk," Roan said. "Fight." He stepped in and feinted with the club and Snaggle-head stepped back heavily, snorting laughter.

"Hey, looks like baby face got hold of some strong sugar-mush." He looked around at the watchers. "What'll we do with him, fellers—"

But Roan's club was whistling, and Snaggle-head jerked back with a yell as the wood smacked solidly against his ribs. He brandished the knife, leaped across a fallen bench; Roan whirled aside, slammed the club hard against the Minid's head. The crewman stumbled, roaring, and rounded on Roan, a line of thick blackish blood inching down his leathery neck. He lunged again and Roan stepped back and brought the club down square across the top of the bald skull. Snaggle-head wheeled, kicked the bench aside, and took up a stance with his feet wide, back bent, arms spread, the blade held across his body. He dashed blood away from his eyes.

"Poundin' my head with that macaroni stick won't buy you nothin', Terry," he grated. His mouth was set in a blue-toothed grin. "I'm comin' to get you now."

He charged and Roan watched the blade swing toward him in a sweeping slash. At the last moment he leaned aside, pivoted, and struck down at the Minid's collarbone; the skrilwood club hit with a sound like an oak branch breaking. Snagglehead yowled and grabbed for his shoulder, spinning away from Roan; his face twisted as he brought the knife up, transferred it with a toss to his left hand.

"Now, I kill you, Terry!"

"You'd better," Roan said, breathing hard. "Because if you don't, I'm going to kill you." Roan moved in, aware of a layer of blue smoke in the muggy air, wide eyes in big Minid faces, the flat shine of Chronid features, the distant putter of a ventilator fan, a puddle of spilled beer under the fallen bench, a smear of dark blood across Snagglehead's cheek. The Minid stood his ground, the knife held before him, its point toward Roan. Roan circled, struck with the club at the knife. The Minid was slow: the blade clattered from the skinned hand, and Roan brought the heavy bludgeon up—

His foot skidded in spilled beer, and he was down, and Snaggle-head was over him, his wide face twisting in a grimace of triumph. The big hands seemed to descend almost casually. Roan threw himself aside, but there were feet and a fallen bench, and the hands clamped on him, biting like grapple hooks, gathering him into a strangling embrace.

He kicked, futile blows against a leg like a tree trunk, hearing the Minid's breath rasp, smelling the chemical reek of Minid blood and Minid hide, and then the arms, thick as Roan's thigh, tightened. Roan's breath went out in a gasp and the smoke and the faces blurred . . .

". . . let him breath a little," Snaggle-head was saying. "Then we'll see how good his eyeballs is hooked on. Then maybe we'll do a little knife work—"

Roan twisted, and the arms constricted.

"Ha, still alive and kicking." Roan felt a big hand grope, find a purchase on his shoulder. He was being held clear of the floor, clamped against the Minid's chest. The Minid's free hand rammed under Roan's chin, forced his face back. A blunt finger bruised his eye.

"Let's start with this one—"

Roan wrenched his head aside, groped with open jaws, found the edge of a hand like a hog-hide glove between his teeth, and bit down with all the force of his jaws. The Minid roared. Roan braced his neck and clung, tasting acrid blood, feeling a bone snap before the hand was torn violently from his grip—

And he struck again, buried his teeth in Snaggle-head's shoulder, grinding a mass of leather-tough muscle, feeling the skin tear as the Minid fell backward.

They were on the floor, Snaggle-head bellowing and striking ineffectually at Roan's back, throwing himself against the scrambling legs of spectators, kicking wildly at nothing. Roan rolled free, came to his knees spitting Minid blood.

"What in the name of the Nine Devils is going on here?" a voice bellowed. Henry Dread pushed his way through the crewmen, stood glaring down at Roan. His eyes went to the groveling crew man.

"What happened to him?" he demanded.

Roan drew breath into his tortured chest. "I'm killing him," he said.

"Killing him, eh?" Henry Dread stared at Roan's white face, the damp red-black hair, the bloody mouth. He nodded, then smiled broadly.

"I guess maybe you're real Terry stock at that, boy. You've got the instinct, all right." He stooped, picked up Snaggle-head's knife, offered it to Roan. "Here, finish him off."

Roan looked at the Minid. The cuts on the bald scalp had bled freely, and more blood from the torn shoulder had spread across the chest. Snaggle-head sat, legs drawn up, cradling his bitten hand and moaning. Tears cut pale paths through the blood on his coarse face.

"No," Roan said.

"What do you mean, no?"

"I don't want to kill him now. I'm finished with him."

Henry Dread held the knife toward Roan. "I said kill him," he grated.

"Get the vet," Roan said. "Sew him up."

Henry stared at Roan. Then he laughed. "No guts to finish what you started, hey?" He tossed the knife to a hulking Chronid, nodded toward Snaggle-head.

"Get the vet!" Roan looked at the Chronid.

"Touch him and I'll kill you," he said, trying not to show how much it hurt to breathe.

In the profound silence, Snaggle-head sobbed.

"Maybe you're right," Henry Dread said. "Alive, he'll be a walking reminder to the rest of the boys. OK, Hulan, get the doc down here." He looked around at the other crewmen.

"I'm promoting the kid to full crew status. Any objections?"

Roan listened, swallowing against a sickness rising up inside him. He walked past Henry Dread, went along the dim way between the high bunks, pushed out into the corridor.

"Hey, kid," Henry Dread said behind him. "You're shaking like a Groac in molting time. Where the hell are your bandages?"

"I've got to get back to my mop," Roan said. He drew a painful breath.

"To hell with the mop. Listen, kid—"

"That's how I earn my food, isn't it? I don't want any charity from you."

"You'd better come along with me, kid," Henry Dread said. "It's time you and me had a little talk."

Foreword to
"The Lawgiver"

Is it enough to be right? Or need we also be fully informed? "To understand all is to forgive all," somebody once said, quite incorrectly. In the name of tolerance should a man condone evil, knowing it to be evil? Should he tolerate filth? Who is to define such terms? Why am I asking these questions? Because to the extent that I can control the minuscule impact I have on the world, I'd like to be sure that my weight is applied on the side of what's good for us. That's often difficult. Many people of good will fall back on a slogan, party-line jargon, simple adages derived from religious, patriotic, or commercial writings.

Senator Eubanks was faced with such a problem. What would you have done? What would I have done? This is what the senator did.

The Lawgiver

"You're no better than a murderer," the woman said. "A cold-blooded killer." Her plump face looked out of the screen at him, hot-eyed, tight-mouthed. She looked like someone's aunt getting tough with the butcher.

"Madam, the provisions of the Population Control Act—" he started.

"That's right, give it a fancy name," she cut in. "Try and make it sound respectable. But that don't change it. It's plain murder. Innocent little babies that never done anybody harm—"

"We are not killing babies! A fetus at ninety days is less than one inch long."

"Don't matter how long they are, they got as much right to live as anybody!"

He drew a calming breath. "In five years we'd be faced with famine. What would you have us do?"

"If you big men in Washington would go to work and provide for people, for the voters, instead of killing babies, there'd be plenty for everybody."

"As easy as that, eh? Does it occur to you, madam, that the land can't support the people if they're swarming over it like ants?"

"See? People are no more to you than ants!"

"People are a great deal more to me than ants! That's precisely why I've sponsored legislation designed to ensure that they don't live like insects, crowded in hives, dying of starvation after they've laid the countryside bare!"

"Look at you," she said, "taking up that whole fancy apartment. You got room there for any number o' homeless children."

"There are too many homeless children, that's the problem!"

"It says right in the Good Book, be fruitful and multiply."

"And where does it end? When they're stacked like cordwood in every available square inch of space?"

"Is that what you do? Heap up all them little bodies and set 'em afire?"

"There are no bodies affected by the law, only fertilized ova!"

"Every one's a human soul!"

"Madam, each time a male ejaculates, several million germ cells are lost. Do you feel we should preserve every one, mature it *in vitro*—"

"Well! You got your nerve, talking that way to a respectable lady! You—a divorced man. And that son of yours—"

"Thank you for calling, madam," he said, and thumbed the blanking control.

"I ain't no madam . . ." The voice died in a squeal. He went to the small bar at the side of the room, dispensed a stiff shot of over-proof SGA, took it down at a gulp. Back at the desk, he buzzed the switchboard.

"Jerry, no more calls tonight."

"Sorry about that last one, Senator. I thought—"

"It's all right. But no more. Not tonight. Not until I've had some sleep."

"Big day, eh, Senator, ramrodding the enabling act through like you did. Uh, by the way, Senator, I just had a flash from Bernie, on the desk. He says there's a party asking for you, says they claim they have to see you—"

"Not tonight, Jerry."

"They mentioned your son, Ron, Senator."

"Yes? What about him?"

"Well, I couldn't say, Senator. But Bernie says they say it's pretty important. But like you said, I'll tell him to tell them not tonight."

"Wait a minute, Jerry. Put this party on."

"Sure, Senator."

The face that appeared was that of a young man with a shaven skull, no eyebrows or lashes. He gazed out of the screen with a bored expression.

"Yes, what is it you want?" the senator demanded, with no attempt to be conciliatory.

The youth tipped his head sideways, pointing. "We've got somebody with us you ought to talk to," he said. "In person."

"I understand you mentioned my son's name."

"We'd better come up."

"If you have something of interest to me, I suggest you tell me what it is."

"You wouldn't like that. Neither would Ron."

"Where is Ron?"

The boy made a vague gesture. "Spy, zek. We tried. It's your rax from here on—"

"Kindly speak standard English. I don't understand you."

The youth turned to someone out of sight; his

mouth moved, but the words were inaudible. He turned back.

"You want us to bring Rink up or not?"

"Who *is* Rink?"

"Rink will tell you all that."

"Very well. Take my car, number 763."

He went to the bar, dispensed another stiff drink, then poured it down the drain. He went to the window, deopaqued it. A thousand feet below, a layer of mist glowed softly from the city lights beneath it, stretching all the way to the horizon 50 miles distant.

When the buzzer sounded he turned, called, "Come in." The door slid back. The boy he had talked to and another came through, supporting between them a plump woman with a pale face. The men were dressed in mismatched vest-suits, many times reused. The woman was wrapped in a long cloak. Her hair was disarranged, so that a long black curl bobbed over the right side of her face. Her visible eye held an expression that might have been fear, or defiance. The men helped her to the low couch. She sank down on it heavily, closed her eyes.

"Well? What's this about Ron?" the senator asked.

The two men moved toward the door. "Ask Rink," one of them said.

"Just a minute! You're not leaving this woman here."

"Better get a medic in, Senator," the shaved lad said.

He looked at her. "Is she ill?" She opened her eyes and pushed her hair out of her face. She was pale, and there were distinct dark hollows under her eyes.

"I'm pregnant," she said in a husky voice. "Awful damn pregnant. And Ron's the father."

He walked slowly across to stand before her. "Have you any proof of that remarkable statement?"

She threw threw the cloak open. Her body looked swollen enough to contain quadruplets.

"I'm not referring to the obvious fact of your condition," he said.

"He's the father, all right."

He turned abruptly, went to the desk, put his finger on the vidscreen key.

"I'm not lying," she said. "The paternity's easy to check. Why would I try to lie?" She was sitting up now; her white fingers dug into the plum-colored cushions.

"I assume you make no claim of a legal marriage contract?"

"Would I be here?"

"You're aware of the laws governing childbirth—"

"Sure. I'm aware of the laws of nature, too."

"Why didn't you report to a PC station as soon as you were aware of your condition?"

"I didn't want to."

"What do you expect me to do?"

"Fix it so I can have the baby—and keep him."

"That's impossible, of course."

"It's your own grandson you're killing!" the woman said quickly. "You can talk about how one of your compulsory abortions is no worse than lancing a boil, but this"—she put her hands against her belly—"this is a baby, Senator. He's alive. I can feel him kicking."

His eyes narrowed momentarily. "Where is Ron?"

"I haven't seen him in six months. Not since I told him."

"Does he know you came here?"

"How would he know?"

He shook his head. "What in God's name do you expect of me, girl?"

"I told you! I want my son—alive!"

He moved away from the desk, noting as he did that the two men had left silently. He started to run his fingers through his hair, jerked his hands down, rammed them in the pockets of his lounging jacket. He turned suddenly to face the girl.

"You did this deliberately—"

"Not without help, I didn't."

"Why? With free anti-pregnancy medication and abort service available at any one of a thousand stations in the city, why?"

"Not just free, Senator—compulsory. Maybe I think the government—a bunch of politicians and bureaucrats—has no right to say who can have a child. Or maybe the pills didn't work. Or maybe I just didn't give a damn. What does it matter now?"

"You're not living naked in the woods now. You're part of a society, and that society has the right to regulate itself."

"And I have a right to have a baby! You didn't give me—or anybody—the right to live! You can't take it away!"

He took a turn up and down the room, stopped before her. "Even if I wanted to help you, what is it you imagine I could do?"

"Get me a birth permit."

"Nonsense. You don't even have a contract, and the qualifications—"

"You can fix it."

"I believe this whole thing is no more than a plot to embarrass me!"

The woman laughed. She threw back her head and screamed laughter. "Ron was right! You're a fool! A cold-blooded old fool! Your own grandson— and you think he's something that was just thought up to annoy you!"

"Stop talking as though this were a living child instead of an illegal embryo!"

Her laughter died away in a half titter, half sob. "It's a funny world we've made for ourselves. In the old days, before we got so Goddamned smart, a man would have been proud and happy to know he had a grandson. He'd look forward to all the things he'd teach him, all the things they'd do together. He'd be a little part of the future that he could see growing, living on after he was dead—"

"That's enough!" He drew a controlled breath and let it out. "Do you realize what you're asking of me?"

"Sure. Save my baby's life. Ron's baby."

His hands opened and closed. "You want me to attempt to deliberately circumvent the laws I've devoted my life to creating!"

"Don't put words to it. Just remember it's a baby's life."

"If I knew where Ron was . . ."

"Yes?"

"We could execute a marriage contract, post-date it. I could manage that. As for a birth permit—" He broke off as the girl's face contorted in an expression like a silent scream.

"Better hurry up," she gasped. "They're coming faster now . . ."

"Good God, girl! Why did you wait until now to bring this to me?"

"I kept hoping Ron would come back."

"I'll have to call a doctor. You know what that means."

"No! Not yet! Find Ron!"

"None of this will help if you're both dead." He keyed the screen, gave terse instructions. "Handle this quietly, Jerry, very quietly," he finished.

"Damn you! I was a fool to come to you!"

"Never mind the hysterics. Just tell me where to start looking for Ron."

"I . . . I don't have any idea."

"Those friends of yours: what about them? Would they know?"

"I promised Limmy and Dan I wouldn't get them mixed up in anything."

He snorted. "And you're asking me to break my oath to the people of this country."

The girl gave him an address. "Don't put them in the middle, Senator. They were pretty decent, bringing me here."

"The obstetrician will be here in a few minutes. Just lie there quietly and try to relax."

"What if you can't find Ron?"

"I suppose you know the answer to that as well as I do."

"Senator—do they really . . . kill the babies?"

"The embryo never draws a breath. Under the legal definition, it's not a baby."

"Oh, Senator—for God's sake, find him!"

He closed the door, shutting off his view of her frightened face.

Red light leaked out through the air baffles above the bright-plated plastic door. At the third ring—he could hear the buzzer through the panel—it opened on a shrill of voices, the rattle and boom of music. Acrid, stale-smelling air puffed in his face. A tall man with an oddly trimmed beard looked at him through mirror-lens contacts. A tendril of reddish smoke curled from the room past his head.

"Uh?"

"I'd like to have a word with Mr. Limberg, please."

"Who?"

"Mr. Limberg. Limmy."

"Uh." The bearded man turned away. Beyond him, strangely costumed figures were dimly visible in the thick crimson fog, standing, sitting, lying on the floor. Some were naked, their shaved bodies decorated with painted patterns. A boy and girl dressed in striped tunics and hose undulated past arm in arm, looking curiously alike. The youth with the shaved head appeared, his mouth drawn down at the corners.

"I need to find Ron in a hurry," the senator snapped, skipping preliminaries. "Can you tell me where he might be?"

"Rink had to blow her tonsils, uh?"

"This is important, Limmy. I have to find him. Seconds may be vital."

The boy pushed his lips in and out. Others had gathered, listening.

"Hey, who's the zek?" someone called.

"It's Eubank."

The youth stepped out, pulled the door shut behind him. "Look, I want no part, follow?"

"All I want is to find Ron. I'm not here to get anyone in trouble. I appreciate what you did for the girl."

"Ron's a pile, as far as I'm concerned. When I saw Rink meant to go through with it, I sent word to him. I didn't know if it reached him or not. But he screened me about half an hour ago. He's on his way here now from Phil."

"Oh the shuttle, I suppose. Good. I can contact him en route—"

"With what for fare? I heard you kept him broke."

"His allowance—never mind. If he's not riding the shuttle, how is he getting here?"

"Car."

"You must be mistaken. His license was lifted last year."

"Yeah. I remember when—and why."

"Are you saying . . . suggesting . . ."

"I'm not saying anything. Just that Ron said he'd be at your place as quick as he could get there."

"I see." He half turned away, turned back to thank the boy. But the door had already closed.

"Please try to understand, Lieutenant," Senator Eubank said to the hard, expressionless face on the screen. "I have reason to believe that the boy is operating a borrowed manually controlled vehicle on the Canada autopike, northbound from Philadelphia, ETD forty minutes ago. He's just received some very shocking news, and he's probably driving at a very high speed. He'll be in an agitated condition, and—"

"You have a description of this vehicle, Senator?"

"No. But surely you have means for identifying a car that's not locked into the system."

"That's correct—but it sometimes takes a few minutes. There are a lot of vehicles on the pike, Senator."

"You understand he's under great stress. The circumstances—"

"We'll take him off as gently as we can."

"And you'll keep me informed? I must see him at the first possible instant, you understand?"

"We'll keep you advised." The police officer turned his head as if looking at someone off-screen.

"This may be something, Senator," he said. "I have a report on a four-seater Supercad at Exit 2983. He took the ramp too fast—he was doing a little over two hundred. He went air-borne and crashed." He paused, listening, then nodded. "Looks like paydirt, Senator. The ID checks on the hot-list out of Philly. And it was on manual control."

The officer used his screamlight to clear a path through the crowd to the spot where the heavy car lay on its side under the arches of the overpass. Two men with cutting torches were crouched on top of it, sending up showers of molten droplets.

"He's alive in there?" Senator Eubank asked.

The lieutenant nodded. "The boys will have him out in a couple of minutes. The crash copter is standing by."

The torches stopped sputtering. The two men lifted the door, tossed it down behind the car. A white-suited medic with a bundle under his arm climbed up and dropped inside. Half a minute later the crane arm at the back of the big police cruiser hoisted the shock-seat clear of the wreck. From the distance of 50 feet, the driver's face was clay-white under the polyarcs.

"It's Ron."

The medic climbed down, bent over the victim as the senator and his escort hurried up.

"How does it look?" the lieutenant asked.

"Not too good. Internals. Skull looks OK. If he's

some rich man's pup, he may walk again—with a new set of innards." The man broke off as he glanced up and saw the civilian beside the officer. "But I wouldn't waste any time taking him in," he finished.

The duty medtech shook his head. "I'm sorry, sir. He's on the table right at this moment. There's no way in the world for you to see him until he comes out. He's in very serious condition, Senator."

"I understand." As the tech turned away, Eubank called after him: "Is there a private screen I could use?"

"In the office, sir."

Alone, he punched his apartment code. The operator's face appeared on the screen. "I'm sorry, no— Oh, it's you, Senator. I didn't know you'd gone out—"

"Buzz my flat, Jerry."

The screen winked and cleared. After 15 seconds' wait, the image of a small, sharp-eyed man appeared, rubbing at his elbows with a towel.

"About time you called in, John," he said. "First time in thirty years I've let myself be hauled out of my home in the midst of dinner."

"How is she?"

The elderly man wagged his head. "I'm sorry, John. She slipped away from me."

"You mean—she's dead?"

"What do you expect? A post-terminal pregnancy—she'd been taking drugs for a week to delay the birth. She'd had no medical attention whatever. And your living room rug doesn't make the best possible delivery table! There was massive hemorrhaging. It might have been different if

I'd been working in a fully equipped labor room, but under the circumstances, that was out of the question, of course, even if there'd been time."

"You know . . . ?"

"The woman told me something of the circumstances."

"What about the child?"

"Child?" The little man frowned. "I suppose you refer to the fetus. It wasn't born."

"You're going to leave it inside the corpse?"

"What would you have me do?" The doctor lowered his voice. "John, is what she said true? About Ron being the father?"

"Yes—I think so."

The little man's mouth tightened. "Her heart stopped three and a half minutes ago. There's still time for a Caesarian, if that's what you want."

"I . . . I don't know, Walter."

"John, you devoted thirty years of your life to the amendment of the enabling act. It passed by a very thin cat's whisker. And the opposition hasn't given up, not by a damn sight. The repeal movement is already underway, and it has plenty of support." The doctor paused, peering at the senator. "I can bring the child out, but John, a lot of this is already in the record. There'd be no way of keeping it out of the hands of the other side: *your* law, violated by you, the first week it was in force. It would finish you, John, and Population Control, too, for a generation."

"There's no hope of resuscitating the mother?"

"None at all. Even today people sometimes die, John."

Foreword to an excerpt from
Night of Delusions

God," *H. L. Mencken declared, "must be a committee," because, he explains, only a committee could have so thoroughly loused up the job of creating the world. Presumably, he thought he could do better. So does practically everyone, including Florin, who, unlike most, had an opportunity to try. I was most interested, as Florin set himself this task, to see how one could 'change this sorry scheme of things entire, and mould it nearer to his heart's desire.'*

Funnily enough, there seemed to be a number of flies, or possibly eagles, in the ointment, and each effort simply to swat these somehow seemed to find the elusive musca domestica *parked on a custard pie.*

A basic characteristic of insanity is the belief, by the victim, that a number of conditions exist, which, in reality, do not exist. If these conditions were met by rearranging reality a bit, would the maniac, by definition, then be sane?

An excerpt from
Night of Delusions

"Nice," I called into the emptiness, "but a trifle stark for my taste. Let there be light!"

And there was light.

And I saw that it was good, and I divided the light from the darkness. It still looked a little empty, so I added a firmament, and divided the waters under it from the waters above it. That gave me an ocean with a lot of wet clouds looking down on it.

"Kind of monotonous," I said. "Let the waters be gathered together off to the side and let's see a little dry land around here."

And it was so.

"Better," I said. "But still dead-looking. Let there be life."

Slime spread across the water and elaborated into seaweed, and clumps floated ashore and lodged there and put out new shoots and crawled up on the bare rocks and sunned itself; and the earth brought forth grass and herbs yielding seeds, and fruit trees and lawns and jungles and flower boxes and herbaceous borders and moss and celery and a lot of other green stuff.

"Too static," I announced. "Let's have some animals."

And the earth brought forth whales and cattle

and fowl and creeping things, and they splashed and mooed and clucked and crept, livening things up a little, but not enough.

"The trouble is, it's too quiet," I pointed out to me. "Nothing's happening."

The earth trembled underfoot and the ground heaved and the top of a mountain blew off and lava belched out and set the forested slopes afire, and the black clouds of smoke and pumice came rolling down on me. I coughed and changed my mind and everything was peaceful again.

"What I meant was something pleasant," I said, "like a gorgeous sunset, with music."

The sky jerked and the sun sank in the south in a glory of purple and green and pink, while chords boomed down from an unseen source in the sky, or inside my head. After it had set I cranked it back up and set it again a few times. Something about it didn't seem quite right. Then I noticed it was the same each time. I varied it and ran through half a dozen more dusks before I acknowledged that there was still a certain sameness to the spectacle.

"It's hard work, making up a new one each time," I conceded. "It gives me a headache. How about just the concert without the light show?"

I played through what I could remember of the various symphonies, laments, concerti, ballads, madrigals, and singing commercials. After a while I ran out. I tried to make up one of my own, but nothing came. That was an area I would have to look into—later. Right now I wanted fun.

"Skiing," I specified. "Healthful exercise in the open air, the thrill of speed!" I was rushing down a slope, out of control, went head over insteps and broke both legs.

"Not like that," I complained, reassembling myself. "No falling down."

I whizzed down the slope, gripped in a sort of invisible padded frame that wrenched me this way and that, insulating me from all shocks.

"Talk about taking a bath in your BVDs," I cried. "I might as well be watching it on TV."

I tried surfing, riding the waves in like the rabbit at a dogtrack, locked to the rails. The surf was all around, but it had nothing to do with me.

"No good. You have to learn how—and that's hard work. Skydiving, maybe?" I gripped the open door frame and stepped out. Wind screamed past me as I hung motionless, watching a pastel-toned tapestry a few feet below grow steadily larger. Suddenly it turned into trees and fields rushing up at me; I grabbed for the ring, yanked—

The jolt almost broke my back. I spun dizzily, swinging like the pendulum of a grandfather clock, and slammed into solid rock.

I was being dragged by the chute. I managed to unbuckle the harness and crawl under a bush to recuperate.

"There's tricks to every trade," I reminded myself, "including being God. What's the point in doing something if I don't enjoy it?" That started me thinking about what I did enjoy.

"It's all yours, old man," I pointed out. "How about a million dollars to start with?"

The bills were neatly stacked, in bundles of $1,000, in tens, twenties, fifties, and hundreds. There were quite a lot of them.

"That's not quite it. What good is money *per se*?

It's what you can buy with it. Like for example, a brand-new 1936 Auburn boat-tailed Speedster, with green leather upholstery."

It was there, parked on the drive. It smelled good. The doors had a nice slam. I cranked up, gunned it up to 50 along the road that I caused to appear in front of it. I went faster and faster: 90 ... 110 ... 200 ... After a while I got tired of buffeting wind and dust in my eyes, and eliminated them. That left the roar and the jouncing.

"You're earthbound," I accused. So I added wings and a prop and was climbing steeply in my Gee Bee Sportster, the wind whipping back past my face bearing a heartening reek of castor oil and high octane. But quite suddenly the stubby racer whip-stalled and crashed in a ploughed field near Peoria. There wasn't enough left of me to pick up with a spoon. I got it together and was in a T-33, going straight up as smooth as silk—30,000 feet ... 40,000 feet ... 50,000 feet. I leveled off and did snap rolls and loops and chandelles and started getting airsick. I sailed down a canyon that followed a sinuous course between heaped clouds, and got sicker. I came in low over the fence, holding her off for a perfect touchdown, and barely made it before I urped.

The trouble is, chum, wherever you go, you're still stuck with yourself. How about a quieter pastime?

I produced a desert isle, furnished it with orchids and palm trees, a gentle breeze, white surf edging the blue lagoon. I built a house of red padauk wood and glass and rough stone high on the side of the central mountain, and I set it about with tropical gardens and ponds and a waterfall, and strolled out on my patio to take my ease beside my pool with a tall cool drink ready to hand. The drink gave me an appetite. I summoned up a table groaning under roast fowl and cold melon and chocolate eclairs and white wine. I ate for a long time; when my appetite began to flag, I whipped it along with shrimp and roast beef and chef salad and fresh pineapple and rice with chicken and sweet-and-sour pork and cold beer. I felt urpy again.

I took a nap in my nine-foot-square bed with silken sheets. After 14 hours' sleep it wasn't comfortable anymore. I ate again, hot dogs and jelly doughnuts this time. It was very filling. I went for a dip in the lagoon. The water was cold and I cut my foot on the coral. Then I got a cramp, luckily in shallow water so that I didn't actually drown. Drowning, I decided, was one of the more unpleasant ways to go.

I limped back up and sat on the beach and thought about my 5,000-tape automatic music system, my 10,000-book library, my antique gun and coin collections, my closets full of hand-woven suits and hand-tooled shoes, my polo ponies, my yacht—

"Nuts," I said. "I get seasick, and don't know how to ride. And what can you do with old coins but look at them? And it'll take me forty years to get through the books. And—"

I suddenly felt tired. But I didn't want to sleep. Or eat. Or swim. Or anything.

"What good is it," I wanted to know, "if you're alone? If there's nobody to show off to, or share it with, or impress, or have envy me? Or even play games with?" I addressed these poignant queries to the sky, but nobody answered, because I had neglected to put anybody up there for the purpose. I thought about doing it, but it seemed like too much effort.

"The trouble with this place is no people," I admitted glumly. "Let there be Man," I said, and created Him in my own image.

The Senator crawled out from under a hibiscus bush and dusted his knees off.

"It was Van Wouk's scheme," he said. "Once you'd decided to go ahead with the simulator project, he said it was only justice that you should be the one to test it. I swear I didn't know he planned to drop you. I was just along for the ride. I was victimized as much as you—"

"My mistake," I said. "Go back where you came from." He disappeared without a backward glance.

"What I really want," I said, "is strangers. People I never saw before, people who won't start in telling me all the things I did wrong."

A small band of Neanderthals emerged from a copse, so intent on turning over logs looking for succulent grubs that they didn't see me at first. Then an old boy with grizzled hair all over him spotted me and barked like a dog and they all ran away.

"I had in mind something a bit more sophisticated," I carped. "Let's have a town, with streets and shops and places where a fellow can get in out of the rain."

The town was there, a straggle of mud-and-wattle huts, bleak under leaden skies. I ordered sunshine, and it broke through the clouds. I made a few improvements in the village, not many or important, just enough to make it homey, and it was Lower

Manhattan on a bright afternoon. The Neanderthals were still there, shaved and wearing clothes, many of them driving cabs, others jostling me on the sidewalk. I went into a bar and took a table on the right side, facing the door, as if I were expecting someone. A fat waitress in a soiled dress two sizes too small came over and sneered at me and fetched her pencil down from behind an ear like a bagel.

I said, "Skip it," waved the whole thing away, and pictured a cozy little fire on the beach with people sitting around it cross-legged, toasting weiners and marshmallows.

"Ah, the simple life," I said, and moved up to join them. They looked up, and a big fellow with a mat of black hair on his chest stood up and said, "Beat it, Jack. Private party."

"I just want to join the fun," I said. "Look, I brought my own weenie."

A girl screamed and Blackie came in fast, throwing lefts and rights, most of which I deftly intercepted with my chin. I went down on my back and got a mouthful of callused foot before I whisked the little group out of existence. I spat sand and tried to appreciate the solitude, the quiet slap of the surf, and the big moon hanging over the water, and might have been making headway, when an insect sank his fangs into that spot under the shoulder blades, the one you can't reach. I eliminated animal life for the moment, and paused for thought.

"I've been going about it wrong. What I want is a spot I fit into; a spot where life is simpler and sweeter, and has a place for me. What better spot than my own past?"

I let my thoughts slide back down the trail to

the memory of a little frame schoolhouse on a dirt road on a summer day, long ago. I was there, eight years old, wearing knickers and sneakers and a shirt and tie, sitting at a desk with an inkwell full of dried ink and covered with carved initials, my hands folded, waiting for the bell to ring. It did, and I jumped up and ran outside into the glorious sunshine of youth. A kid three sizes bigger, with bristly red hair, scrubbed his knuckles rapidly back and forth across my scalp, and threw me down and jumped on me, and I felt my nose start to bleed.

So I wrapped him in chains, dropped a 17-ton trip-hammer on him, and was alone again.

"That was all wrong," I said. "That wasn't the idea at all. That wasn't facing real life, with all its joys and sorrows. That was a cop-out. To mean anything, the other guy has to have a chance. It has to be man to man, the free interplay of personality—that's what makes for the rich, full life."

I made myself six feet three and magnificently muscled, with crisp golden curls and a square jaw, and Pig Eyes came out of an alley with a length of pipe and smashed the side of my head in. I dressed myself in armor with a steel helmet, and he came up behind me and slipped a dirk in through the chink where my gorget joined my epauliere. I threw the armor away, slipped into my black belt, went into a *neko-ashi-dashi* stance and ducked his slash. He shot me through the left eye.

I blanked it all out and was back on the beach— just me and the skeeters.

"That's enough acting on impulse," I told myself sternly. "Hand-to-hand combat isn't really your idea of fun; if you lose, it's unpleasant; and if you always win, why bother?"

I didn't have a good answer for that one. That encouraged me, so I went on: "What you really want is companionship, not rivalry. Just the warmth of human society on a noncompetitive basis."

At once, I was the center of a throng. They weren't doing anything much, just thronging. Warm, panting bodies, pressed close to me. I could smell them. That was perfectly normal—bodies do have smells. Someone stepped on my foot and said, "Excuse me." Somebody else stepped on my other foot and didn't say excuse me. A man fell down and died. Nobody paid any attention. I might not have either, except that the man was me. I cleared the stage and sat on the curb and watched the sad city sunlight shine down on a scrap of paper blowing along the sidewalk. It was a dead, dirty city. On impulse, I cleaned it up, even to removing the grime from the building fronts.

That made it a dead, clean city.

"The ultimate in human companionship," I thought to myself, "is that of a desirable and affectionate female of nubile years and willing disposition."

Accordingly, I was in my penthouse apartment; the hi-fi was turned low, the wine was chilled, and she was reclining at ease on the commodious and cushion-scattered chaise longue. She was tall, shapely, with abundant reddish-brown hair, smooth skin, large eyes, a small nose. I poured. She wrinkled her nose at the wine and yawned. She had nice teeth.

"Golly, haven't you got any groovy records?"

she asked. Her voice was high, thin, and self-indulgent.

"What would you prefer?"

"I dunno. Something catchy." She yawned again and looked at the heavy emerald and diamond bracelet on her wrist.

"Come on, really," she said. "How much did it cost?"

"I got it free. I have a pal in the business. It's a demonstrator."

She took it off and threw it on the inch-thick rug. "I've got this terrible headache," she whined. "Call me a cab."

"That shows what you really think of the kind of girls who go with penthouses and hi-fi," I told myself, dismissing her with a wave of my hand. "What you really want is a homey girl, sweet and innocent and unassuming."

I came up the steps of the little white cottage with the candle in the window and she met me at the door with a plate of cookies. She chattered about her garden and her sewing and her cooking as we dined on corn bread and black-eyed peas with lumps of country ham in it. Afterward she washed and I dried. Then she tatted while I sat by the fire and oiled harness or something of the sort. After a while she said, "Well, good night," and left the room quietly. I waited five minutes and followed. She was just turning back the patchwork quilt; she was wearing a thick woolen nightgown, and her hair was in braids.

"Take it off," I said. She did. I looked at her. She looked like a woman.

"Uh, let's go to bed," I said. We did.

"Don't you have anything to say?" I wanted to know.

"What shall I say?"

"What's your name?"

"You didn't give me one."

"You're Charity. Where are you from, Charity?"

"You didn't say."

"You're from near Dothan. How old are you?"

"Forty-one minutes."

"Nonsense! You're at least, ah, twenty-three. You've lived a full, happy life, and now you're here with me, the culmination of all your dreams."

"Yes."

"Is that all you have to say? Aren't you happy? Or sad? Don't you have any ideas of your own?"

"Of course. My name is Charity, and I'm twenty-three, and I'm here with you—"

"What would you do if I hit you? Suppose I set the house on fire? What if I said I was going to cut your throat?"

"Whatever you say."

I got a good grip on my head and suppressed a yell of fury.

"Wait a minute, Charity—this is all wrong. I didn't mean you to be an automaton, just mouthing what I put in your head. Be a real, live woman. React to me—"

She grabbed the covers up to her chin and screamed.

I sat in the kitchen alone and drank a glass of cold milk and sighed a lot.

"Let's think this thing through," I suggested. "You can make it any way you want it. But you're trying to do it too fast; you're taking too many shortcuts. The trick is to start slowly, build up the details, make it real."

So I thought up a small Midwestern city, with wide brick streets of roomy old frame houses under big trees, with shady yards and gardens that weren't showplaces, just the comfortable kind where you can swing in a hammock and walk on the grass and pick the flowers without feeling like you're vandalizing a set piece.

I walked along the street, taking it all in, getting the feel of it. It was autumn, and someone was burning leaves somewhere. I climbed the hill, breathing the tangy evening air, being alive. The sound of a piano softly played floated down across the lawn of the big brick house at the top of the hill. Purity Atwater lived there. She was only 17, and the prettiest girl in town. I had an impulse to turn in right then, but I kept going.

"You're a stranger in town," I said. "You have to establish yourself, not just barge in. You have to meet her in the socially accepted way, impress her folks, buy her a soda, take her to the movies. Give her time. Make it real."

A room at the Y cost 50 cents. I slept well. The next morning I applied for work at only three places before I landed a job at two dollars a day at Siegal's Hardware and Feed. Mr. Siegal was favorably impressed with my frank, open countenance, polite and respectful manner, and apparent eagerness for hard work.

After three months, I was raised to $2.25 per day, and took over the bookkeeping. In my room at the boardinghouse I kept a canary and a shelf of inspirational volumes. I attended divine service regularly, and contributed one dime per week to the collection plate. I took a night class in advanced accountancy, sent away for Charles Atlas' course, and allowed my muscles to grow no more than could be accounted for by dynamic tension.

In December I met Purity. I was shoveling snow from her father's walk when she emerged from the big house looking charming in furs. She gave me a smile. I treasured it for a week, and schemed to be present at a party attended by her. I dipped punch for the guests. She smiled at me again. She approved of my bronzed good looks, my curly hair, my engaging grin, my puppylike clumsiness. I asked her to the movies. She accepted. On the third date I held her hand briefly. On the tenth I kissed her cheek. Eighteen months later, while I was still kissing her cheek, she left town with the trumpeter from a jazz band I had taken her to hear.

Undaunted, I tried again. Hope Berman was the second prettiest girl in town. I wooed her via the same route, jumped ahead to kisses on the lips after only 21 dates, and was promptly called to an interview with Mr. Berman. He inquired as to my intentions. Her brothers, large men all, also seemed interested. A position with Berman and Sons, Clothiers, was hinted at. Hope giggled. I fled.

Later, in my room, I criticized myself sternly. I was ruined in Pottsville: word was all over town that I was a trifler. I took my back wages, minus some vague deductions, and with a resentful speech from Mr. Siegal about ingrates and grasshoppers, traveled by train to St. Louis. There I met and paid court to Faith, a winsome lass who worked as a secretary in the office of a lawyer whose name was painted on a second-story window on a side street a few blocks from the more affluent business section. We went to movies, took long streetcar rides, visited museums, had picnics. I noticed that she perspired moderately in warm weather, had several expensive cavities, was ignorant of many matters, and was a very ordinary lay. And afterward she cried and chattered of marriage.

Omaha was a nicer town. I holed up at the Railroad Men's Y there for a week and thought it through. It was apparent I was still acting too hastily. I wasn't employing my powers correctly. I had exchanged the loneliness of God for the loneliness of Man, a pettier loneliness but no less poignant. The trick, I saw, was to combine the highest skills of each status, to live a human life, nudged here and there in the desired direction.

Inspired, I repaired at once to the maternity ward of the nearest hospital, and was born at 3:27 A.M. on a Friday, a healthy, seven-pound boy whom my parents named Melvin. I ate over 400 pounds of Pablum before my first taste of meat and potatoes. Afterward I had a stomach ache. In due course I learned to say bye-bye, walk, and pull tablecloths off tables in order to hear the crash of crockery. I entered kindergarten, and played sand blocks in the band, sometimes doubling in triangle, which was chrome-plated and had a red string. I mastered shoe-tying, pants-buttoning, and eventually rollerskating and falling off my bike. In Junior High I used my 20 cents lunch money for a mayonnaise sandwich, an RC Cola—half of which I squirted at the ceiling and my classmates—and an O'Henry. I read many dull books by Louisa May Alcott and G. A. Henty, and picked out Patience Froomwell as my intended.

She was a charming redhead with freckles. I

took her to proms, picking her up in my first car, one of the early Fords, with a custom body hand-built from planks. After graduation, I went to college, maintaining our relationship via mail. In the summers we saw a lot of each other in a non-anatomical sense.

I received my degree in business administration, secured a post with the power company, married Patience, and fathered two nippers. They grew up, following much the same pattern as I had, which occasioned some speculation on my part as to how much divine intervention had had to do with my remarkable success. Patience grew less and less like her name, gained weight, developed an interest in church work and gardens and a profound antipathy for everyone else doing church work and gardening.

I worked very hard at all this, never yielding to the temptation to take shortcuts, or to improve my lot by turning Patience into a movie starlet or converting our modest six-roomer into a palatial estate in Devon. The hardest part was sweating through a full 60 seconds of subjective time in every minute, 60 minutes every hour. . . .

After 50 years of conscientious effort, I ended up with a workbench in the garage.

At the local tavern, I drank four Scotches and pondered my dilemna. After five Scotches I became melancholy. After six I became defiant. After seven, angry. At this point the landlord was so injudicious as to suggest I had had enough. I left in high dudgeon, pausing only long enough to throw a fire bomb through the front window. It made a lovely blaze. I went along the street fire-bombing the beauty parlor, the Christian Science Reading

Room, the optometrist, the drug store, the auto parts house, the Income Tax Prepared Here place.

"You're all phonies," I yelled. "All liars, cheats, fakes!"

The crowd that had gathered labored and brought forth a policeman, who shot me and three innocent bystanders. This annoyed me even in my exhilarated mood. I tarred and feathered the officious fellow, then proceeded to blow up the courthouse, the bank, the various churches, the supermarket, and the automobile agency. They burned splendidly.

I rejoiced to see the false temples going up in smoke, and toyed briefly with the idea of setting up my own religion, but at once found myself perplexed with questions of dogma, miracles, fund drives, canonicals, tax-free real estate, nunneries, and inquistions, and shelved the idea.

All Omaha was blazing nicely now; I moved on to other cities, eliminating the dross that had clogged our lives. Pausing to chat with a few survivors in the expectation of overhearing expressions of joy and relief at the lifting of the burden of civilization, and praise of the new-found freedom to rebuild a sensible world, I was dismayed to see they seemed more intent on tending their wounds, competing in the pursuit of small game, and looting TV sets and cash, than in philosophy.

By now the glow of the Scotch was fading. I saw I had been hasty. I quickly reestablished order, placing needful authority in the hands of outstanding Liberals. Since there was still a vociferous body of reactionaries creating unrest and interfering with the establishment of total social justice, it was necessary to designate certain personnel to keep order, dressing them in uniform garments, for ease of identification.

Alas, mild policies failed to convince the wreckers that the People meant business and were not to be robbed of the fruits of their hard-won victory over the bloodsuckers. Sterner measures were of necessity resorted to. Still the stubborn Fascists took advantage of their freedom to agitate, make inflammatory speeches, print disloyal books, work hard at their jobs, and in other ways interfere with their comrades' fight for peace and plenty. Temporary controls were accordingly placed on treasonous talk, and exemplary executions were carried out. The burden of these duties proving onerous, I supplied assistant leaders, who found it necessary to retire to the more spacious estates surviving the holocaust, and to limit their diets to caviar, champagne, breast of chicken and other therapeutic items in order to keep up their strength for the battle against reaction. Malcontents naturally attributed the leaders' monopoly on limousines, palaces, custom tailoring, and the company of trained nurses of appearance calculated to soothe the weary executive eye as evidence of decadence. Picture their fury and frustration when the State, refusing to tolerate sedition, bustled them off to remote areas where by performing useful labor under simple conditions, they received an opportunity to correct their thinking.

I called on the Prime Leader—affectionately known as the Dictator—and queried him as to his intentions now that he had consolidated the economy, rooted out traitors, and established domestic tranquility.

"I'm thinking about taking over the adjacent continent," he confided.

"Are they bothering us?" I inquired.

"You bet. Every time I see a good-looking broad on their side of the line and realize she's out of reach . . ." He ground his teeth.

"Joking aside," I persisted. "Now that we have peace—"

"Next thing you know the mob will be getting restless," he said. "Wanting TV sets, cars, iceboxes, even refrigerators! Just because I and my boys have a few little amenities to help us over the intolerable burdens of leadership, they want to get into the act! What do those bums know about the problems we got? Did they ever have to mobilize along a frontier? Did they ever have to make up their minds: 'tanks or tractors'? Do they have to worry about the old international prestige? Not those bums! All they got to worry about is getting through enough groceries to stay alive long enough to have enough brats so there'll be somebody around to bury 'em—as if that was important."

I thought about it. I sighed. "I can't quite put my finger on it," I told the Dictator, "but there's something lacking. It isn't exactly the Utopia I had in mind." I wiped him out and all his works and contemplated the desolation sadly. "Maybe the trouble was I let too many cooks into the broth," I reflected. "Next time I'll set the whole thing up, complete, just the way I like it—and then turn everybody loose in it."

It was a jolly thought. I did it. I turned the wilderness into a parkland, drained the bogs, planted flowers. I set up towns at wide intervals, each a jewel of design, with cozy dwellings and graceful trees and curving paths and fountains and reflecting pools and open-air theaters that fit into the landscape as if a part of it. I set up clean, well-lighted schools and swimming pools, dredged the rivers and stocked them with fish, provided abundant raw materials and a few discreet, well-concealed, nonpolluting factories to turn out the myriad simple, durable, miraculous devices that took all the drudgery out of life, leaving humans free for the civilities that only humans can perform, such as original research, art, massage, and prostitution, plus waiting on tables. Then I popped the population into the prepared setting and awaited the glad cries that would greet the realization that everything was perfect.

Somehow, there seemed to be a certain indifference right from the beginning. I asked a beautiful young couple strolling through a lovely park beside a placid lake if they weren't having a good time.

"I guess so," he said.

"There's nothing to do," she said.

"Think I'll take a nap," he said.

"You don't love me anymore," she said.

"Don't bug me," he said.

"I'll kill myself," she said.

"That'll be the day," he said, and yawned.

"You son of a bitch," she said.

I moved on. A child with golden curls a lot like mine was playing by the lake. She was drowning a kitten. It was just as well; she had already poked its eyes out. I resisted an impulse to tumble the tot in after the cat and approached an old gentleman with cherubic white locks who was standing on a stone bench, peering bemusedly at a large shrub.

At close range I saw he was peering through the shrub at the two nubile maidens disporting themselves naked on the grass. He spun when he heard me coming.

"Scandalous," he quavered. "They've been doing that to each other for the better part of two hours, right out in public where a body can't help seeing them. Makes a body wonder if there aren't enough males to go around."

I had a moment of panic; had I overlooked that detail?

But no, of course not. Male and female created i Them. It was something else that was wrong.

"I know," i cried. "i've been doing too much for Them; They're spoiled. What they need is a noble enterprise that They can tackle together, a brave crusade against the forces of evil, with the Banners of Right floating overhead!"

We were arrayed in ranks, myself at the head, my loyal soldiery behind me. I rose in my stirrups and pointed to the walls of the embattled town ahead.

"There they are, lads," I cried. "The enemy—the killers, looters, rapists, vandals. Now's the time to Get them! Forward once more into the breach, dear friends, for Harry, England, and St. George!"

We charged, battered our way through the defenses. They surrendered; we rode triumphant into the city's streets. My lads leaped from their horses, and began hacking at civilians, smashing windows, and grabbing handfuls of costume jewelery, TV sets, and liquor. They raped all the females, sometimes killing them afterward and sometimes before. They set fire to what they couldn't eat, drink, or screw.

"God has won a glorious victory," my priests cried.

It annoyed me to have my name taken in vain; i caused a giant meteorite to crash down in the midst of the revelry. The survivors cited their survival as evidence of God's approval. I sent a plague of stinging flies, and half the people burned the other half at the stake to appease Me. I sent a flood; they floated around, clinging to fragments of church pews, old TV chassis, and the swollen carcasses of dead cows, horses, and evangelists, yelling for help and making promises to me as to how they would behave if they only got out of this one.

I rescued a few and to my delight they set to work at once to save others, whom they immediately formed into platoons, congregations, labor unions, mobs, crowds, lobbies, and political parties. Each group at once attacked another group, usually the one most similar to themselves. I gave a terrible yell and swept them all away under a tidal wave. The foaming of the waters around the ruins of temples, legislatures, courthouses, clip joints, chemical factories, and the headquarters of the large corporations amused me; I made bigger and better tidal waves, and washed away slums, eroded farmland, burned-off forest areas, silted-up rivers, and polluted seas. Adrenalin flooded my system; my lust to destroy was aroused. I pulverized the continents, shattered the crust, splashed around in the magma that boiled forth.

The moon caught my eye, riding aloof above my wrath. The bland smoothness of it annoyed Me; i threw a handful of gravel at it, pocking the surface nicely. I grabbed the planet Oedipus and threw it at Saturn; it missed, but the close passage broke it up. Major chunks of rock went into orbit around Saturn and the dust formed rings; a few scraps were captured by Mars; the rest trailed off around the sun.

I found that a satisfying spectacle, and turned to invite others to admire it, but of course there was no one there.

"This is the trouble with being god," i groaned. "I could set up a bunch of nincompoops to praise me, but what good is that? A fellow wants a response from an equal, dammit!"

Suddenly i was sick and tired of the whole thing. It should have been easy, when you have all the power there is, to make things the way you want them, but it wasn't. Part of the trouble was that i didn't really know what i wanted, and another part was that i didn't know how to achieve what i wanted when i did know what it was, and another part was that when i got what i thought i wanted it turned out not to be what i wanted. It was too hard, too complicated, being god. It was a lot easier just being a Man. There was a limit on a Man's abilities, but there was also a limit on His responsibilities.

"What i mean is," I told myself, "I'm only a Human Being, no matter what kind of thunderbolts I can throw. I need a few hundred thousand years more evolution, and then maybe I can handle being god."

I stood—or floated, or drifted—in the midst of the Ylem that was all that was left of all my efforts, and remembered Van Wouk and Lard Face and their big plans for me. They weren't sinister anymore, only pathetic. I remembered Diss, the lizard man, and how frightened he had been just at the last. I thought of the Senator, his cowardice and his excuses, and suddenly he seemed merely human. And then I thought about me, and what a shabby figure I had cut, not just as god, but as a Man.

"You looked pretty good in there," i told Me, "up to a point. You're all right as a loser, but you're a lousy winner. Having it all your way is the real problem. Success is the challenge nobody's ever met. Because no matter how many you win, there's always a bigger and harder and more complicated problem ahead, and there always will be, and the secret isn't Victory Forever but to keep on doing the best you can one day at a time and remember you're a Man, not just god, and for you there aren't and never will be any easy answers, only questions, and no reasons, only causes, and no meaning, only intelligence, and no destination, and no kindly magic smiling down from above, and no fires to goad you from below, only Yourself and the Universe and what You make out of the interface between the two equals."

And I rested from all my work which i had made.

Foreword to an excerpt from
The Star Treasure

I have been asked many strange questions by fans (and others). The commonest are:

Q: *Do you believe in flying Saucers?* **A:** *No.*

Q: *Do you drawr the pitchers on the cover?* **A:** *No.*

Q: *Why don't you write something serious?* **A:** *Everything I write is serious, though not solemn.*

But there was one query which, by the scope of its idiocy, the depth of its dumbness, and the profundity of its ignorance, left me (briefly) speechless:

"Do you ever put any of your own ideas in your books?"

One of the ideas I put in a book (yes, Virginia, I do put my own ideas in my books, since they're right there, accessible) is that society has no right, in prescribing punishments for transgressors, to take away anything which it did not confer in the first place. Very well, then: what does society confer, and what can it take back? Midshipman Blane found out.

An excerpt from
The Star Treasure

Midshipman Blane was cashiered at 0800 hours on Sarday, Ma 35, 2190, on the parade deck of the ship of the line *Tyrant*, 50 million tons, on station off Callisto, nine months out of Terra on the Trans-Jovian cruise.

Blane was a slim, sandy-haired lad only a year out of the Academy. He stood obediently at attention while the commodore read the findings of the court: guilty of attempted sabotage in that he did willfully place and attempt to detonate an explosive device with the intention of destroying a capital Fleet vessel on active patrol in Deep Space.

"In an earlier age," the commodore went on, "a terrible vengeance would have been extracted from a man who undertook, however ineffectually, the destruction of his ship and the murder of eighteen thousand shipmates. Today the law holds that society may legitimately exact only those punishments commensurate with its ability to confer benefits.

"Charles Yates Blane, society has reposed confidence in your abilities and integrity; that confidence is now withdrawn. Society has conferred on you rank and responsibility; of that rank and those responsibilities you are now relieved. Society has endowed you with citizenship and the privileges of

240

participating in her benefits; those privileges are now revoked. You are no longer a member of the United Planetary Navy, nor have you the right to wear the uniform."

At a command the drummers started the roll. The commodore grasped the insignia on the midshipman's collar and ripped it away. He stripped the single gold stripe from his cuff. He snapped off the ornamental silver buttons with the Fleet eagle, one by one, and dropped them at his feet.

Blane didn't move, except to sway a little at each jerk, but tears were running down his face.

The drums halted. In the aching silence, the vice-Commodore said, "Charles Blane, ex-officer, ex-citizen, you will now be removed to a place of security and held there until the arrival of a Fleet picket boat which will transport you to a designated location where you will be free to work out your destiny unassisted, and unimpeded, by the society which you have forfeited."

For the first time, a trace of emotion showed on the Commodore's face: the faintest of sneers—all that was left to a civilized man of the bared fangs of the ancestral carnivore.

"Take him away," he said. The drummers resumed the roll; the guard closed in, fore and aft, and walked him down the gauntlet of the men and women he'd tried to kill, and out of our lives.

Foreword to an excerpt from
The Long Twilight

A machine, built long ago, lies dormant but aware, as ages pass, until the programmed moment arrives; then it begins to function, though its long-gone builders had forgotten it millennia ago.

Two men, strangely alike, respond in bewilderment, and gradually the fate that links them draws them to a confrontation. Start with that, and discover what happens as the long twilight—the Gotterdämmerung, slowly falls.

This is the episodic type of novel, with many strands to weave into a pattern that, for me, is the most challenging, and each day while the work is in progress, I'm eager to get back to it, to discover what will happen next. It's true that a well-conceived story takes on a life of its own, and is not to be confined to the restrictions of an outline.

An excerpt from
The Long Twilight

A man sat at a small desk beside an open window, writing with an old-fashioned steel-nib pen which he dipped at intervals into a pot of blue-black ink. A soft sea-wind moved the curtain, bringing an odor of salt and kelp. Far away, a bell chimed out the hour of six P.M.

The man wrote a line, crossed it out, sat looking across the view of lawns and gardens. His face was strong-featured, square-jawed. His gray hair lay close to a finely formed skull. His fingers were thick, square-tipped; powerful fingers.

"Writing pomes again, Mr. Grayle?" A voice spoke suddenly from the doorway behind the man. He turned with a faint smile.

"That's right, Ted." His voice was deep, soft, with a faint trace of accent.

"You like to write pomes, don't you, Mr. Grayle?" Ted grinned in mild conspiracy.

"Um-hum."

"Hey, game time, Mr. Grayle. Guess you maybe didn't hear the bell."

"I guess not, Ted." Grayle rose.

"Boy oh boy, the Blues are going to mop up on the Reds tonight, hey, Mr. Grayle?" Ted stood aside as Grayle stepped out into the wide, well-lit corridor.

"Sure we will, Ted."

They walked along the passage, where other men were emerging from rooms.

"Well, tonight's the night, eh, Mr. Grayle?" Ted said.

"Tonight?" Grayle inquired mildly.

"You know. The new power system goes on. Just pick it out of the air. Nifty, huh?"

"I didn't know."

"You don't read the papers much, do you, Mr. Grayle?"

"Not much, Ted."

"Boy oh boy." Ted waggled his head. "What will they come up with next?"

They crossed an airy court, passed through an arcade, and emerged onto a wide, grassy meadow. Men dressed in simple, well-made, one-piece garments, some bearing a red armband, others a blue, stood in groups talking, tossing a baseball back and forth.

"Go get 'em, Mr. Grayle," Ted said. "Show 'em the old stuff."

"That's right, Ted."

The man called Ted leaned against a column, arms folded, watched as Grayle walked across to join his team.

"Hey, that's the guy, huh?" A voice spoke beside Ted. He turned and gave an up-and-down frown to the young fellow who had come up beside him.

"What guy?"

"The mystery man. I been hearing about him. Nobody knows how long he's been here. I heard he killed a guy with an ax. He doesn't look like so much to me."

"Mr. Grayle is an all-right guy, greenhorn," Ted said. "That's a lot of jetwash about nobody knows how long he's been here. They got records. They know, OK."

"How long you been here, Ted?"

"Me? Five years, why?"

"I talked to Stengel; he came here nineteen years ago. He says the guy was here then."

"So?"

"He doesn't look old enough to be an old con."

"What's he supposed to look, old? So he's maybe thirty-five, maybe forty-five. So what?"

"I'm curious, is all."

"Hah," Ted said. "You college-trained guys. You got too many theories."

The young fellow shrugged. The two guards stood watching as the teams formed up for the nightly ball game played by the inmates of the Caine Island Federal Penitentiary.

2

It was a long, narrow room, dim, age-grimed, smelling of the spilled beers of generations. Weak late-afternoon sunshine filtered through the bleary plate-glass window where garish blue glow-letters spelled out *Fangio's* in reverse. A man with four chins and a bald skull bulked behind the bar, talking to a small, quick-eyed man who hunched on a stool next to a defunct jukebox loaded with curled records five years out of date. In the corner booth, a man with a badly scarred face sat talking to himself. He was dressed in an expensive gray suit which was dusty and stained. A gold watch gleamed on one wrist, visible under a black-edged cuff as he gesticulated.

"The bum is dough-heavy," the small man said, watching the lone drinker in the tarnished mirror through a gap in the clutter of blended-whiskey bottles on the backbar. "Did you eyeball that bundle?"

Fangio's eyes moved left, right, left, as he scraped slops onto a chipped plate.

"Seen Soup around, Lou?" he murmured.

The small man's eyelids flickered an affirmative.

Fangio laid the plate aside and wiped his hands on his vest.

"I got to go out back," he said. "Keep an eye on the place." He walked away, eased sideways through a narrow door. The small man went to the phone booth at the end of the bar and punched keys; he talked, watching the scarred man.

A woman came in through the black-glass doors. She was middle-aged, a trifle plump, heavily made up. She took a stool at the bar, looked around, and called, "OK, snap it up. The lady's waiting."

The small man kicked open the door of the booth.

"Beat it, Wilma," he said in a low urgent voice. "Fangio ain't in."

"What're you, the night watchman?"

"Go on, dust," Lou snapped.

The woman twisted her mouth at him. "I'll get my own." She started around behind the bar. The small man jumped to her, caught her bracelet-heavy arm, twisted savagely. She yelped and kicked at him.

The doors banged as a squat man in a shapeless gray coverall came in. He stopped dead, looking at the two. He had a wide, dark face, bristly black hair; acne scars pitted his jaw and hairline.

"What the—" he started.

"Yeah, Soup," the small man said. "I was calling ya." He stepped clear of the woman, who snorted and yanked at her dress. The small man tipped his head, indicating the occupied booth.

Soup gave Wilma a deadly look. "Beat it," he said. She scuttled behind him and out the door.

In the booth, the scarred man was opening and closing his fist.

". . . golden bird of Ahuriel," he said. "Once flown, never to be recaptured . . ."

"What's he talking about?" Soup asked.

The small man shook his head. "He's scrambled." They walked back, stopped beside the table. The scarred man ignored them.

"Try the left hip," Lou suggested.

Soup reached out, with a practiced motion took the drunk's arm up behind him, forcing his face down onto the table. A glass fell over. Soup reached across behind the seated man, patted his back pocket, brought out a sheaf of currency, folded once across the middle. The bill on the outside was a fifty. Holding the owner's arm, he spread the bills.

"Hey," he said. "New shoes for baby."

He released the seated man's arm and stepped back. The victim sprawled, unmoving, with his cheek against the table.

They had taken two steps when the scarred man came up out of the booth in a lunge, locked his arm across the squat man's throat, and bent him backward.

"Stay, hagseed!" he hissed. His face was mottled,

blurred, contorted. "Art *his* emissaries? Lurks *he* yonder?"

The small man made a grab for the money still in his partner's hand, missed, turned, and ran for the door.

"Find thy tongue, wretch, ere my dirk slits thy weasand!"

Soup's hand, clutching the money, waved near the scarred man's face; he plucked the bills away, as with a desperate plunge the squat man broke free.

"Stay, whelp, I'll have report o' thy master!" the scarred man snarled, making a grab at the man. He missed, staggered against a booth. The squat man disappeared via the rear door. The scarred man looked at the money in his hand as though noticing it for the first time.

"Nay . . . 'twere but a mere cutpurse," he muttered. "Naught more . . ." He looked around as the door opened cautiously. The woman called Wilma looked in, came through.

"Hey," she said. "What gives?"

The scarred man blinked at her, weaving.

"Fetch ale, wench," he muttered, and turned, half-fell into the nearest seat.

The rear door burst open; Fangio appeared, goggling.

"Hey, what—"

"Draw two," the woman barked. She sat down across from the scarred man, who was leaning back, eyes shut, mouth open. She stared curiously at his disfigurements.

"You know him?" Fangio asked tersely.

"Sure. Him and me are old pals." She transferred her gaze to the money in the drunken man's hand.

"*Varför?*" the scarred man mumbled. "*Varför har du gjört det, du som var min vän och brör?*"

"Why does he talk funny?" Fangio was frowning darkly.

"He's some kind of a Dane," the woman said quickly. "My first husband was a Dane. I heard plenty of that kind of jabber."

"He looks like some kind of Jew," Fangio said.

"Get the beers," the woman said. "You ain't no Jew, are you, honey?" She patted the big-knuckled hand that lay on the table.

"Geez, will you look at them scars?" Fangio said.

"Used to be a fighter," the woman said. "What is this, a quiz show?"

" 'Twere but a dream," the scarred man said suddenly. He opened his eyes, looked vaguely at the woman.

"Just . . . dream," he said. "That's all. Bad dream. Forget it."

The woman patted his hand again. "Sure, honey. Forget it. Wilma will take care of you. Wilma's got a room, honey. We better get you there while you can still navigate. . . ."

3

At the Upper Shoshone Generating Station (Experimental), a dozen senators and representatives, the state governor, assorted lesser political lights, and a selected cadre of reporters were grouped around the Secretary of the Interior as he stood chatting with the chief engineer and his top aides before the 40-foot-wide, 12-foot-high panel clustered thick with instrument dials and aflash with reassuring amber, red, and green lights, indicating that all was in readiness for the first commercial transmission of beamed power in the history of the Republic.

"It's impressive, Mr. Hunnicut," the Secretary said, nodding. "A great achievement."

"If it works," a saintly-looking senator said sharply.

"The technical people assure us that it will, Cy," the Secretary said tolerantly.

"I'm familiar with the inverse square law," the senator retorted. "You go pouring power out into the air, not one percent of it will get where it's supposed to go. It's a boondoggle! A waste of the taxpayers' money."

The chief engineer frowned as the reporters jotted briskly.

"Senator, I don't think you quite understand. We aren't broadcasting power as you call it— not directly. We erect a carrier field—somewhat similiar to the transmission of a Three-V broadcast. When the field impinges on a demand point—an energy-consuming device, that is, of the type responsive to the signal—there's a return impulse, an echo—"

"The senator knows all that, Mr. Hunnicut," the Secretary said, smiling indulgently. "He's speaking for publication."

A man in an oil-spotted smock came up, showed the chief engineer a clipboard. He nodded, looked at the clock on the antiseptically white wall.

"Two minutes to zero hour," the Secretary said. "Everything is still proceeding normally?"

"Yes, sir, Mr. Secretary," the technician said,

then retreated under the blank look this netted him from the dignitary.

"All systems are functioning," Hunnicut said, making it official. "I see no reason that we shouldn't switch over on schedule."

"Think of it, gentlemen." The Secretary turned to the legislators and, incidentally, to the reporters. "Raw power, torn from the heart of the atom, harnessed here, waiting the call that will send it pouring into the homes and factories of America—"

"At this point, we're only powering a few government-operated facilities and public-utilities systems," Hunnicut interjected. "It's still a pilot operation."

". . . freeing man from his age-old drudgery, ushering in a new era of self-realization and boundless promise—"

"Sixty seconds," a voice spoke sharply from a ceiling grill. "Automatic hold."

"Proceed," Hunnicut said.

In silence the men stood watching as the second hand of the big clock scythed away the final minute of an era.

4

The scarred man lay on his back on the narrow bed, sleeping with his mouth open. His face, in the slack repose of profound drunkenness, was a ravaged field where battles had been fought, and lost, long ago.

The woman called Wilma stood beside the bed, watching him by the glow of a shadeless table lamp. She tensed as the light faltered, dimmed. Shadows closed in on the shabby room; then the lamp winked back to full brightness. The woman let out the breath she had been holding, her momentary panic dissipating.

"Sure, it said on the tube about switching over onto the new radio power tonight," she murmured half-aloud. On the bed, the scarred man stiffened; he grimaced, moving his head from side to side. He groaned, sighed, grew still again.

Wilma leaned over him. Her hands moved deftly, searching out his pockets. They were empty, but she found the rolls of bills wadded under the folded blanket that served as a pillow. As she withdrew it, she glanced at his face. He eyes were wide open, locked on hers.

"I . . . I was just fixing your pillers," she said.

He sat up with an abruptness that sent her stumbling away, clutching the money in her hand.

"I . . . I was going to take care of it for you." Even in her own ears, her voice sounded as false as brass jewelry.

He looked away, shaking his head vaguely. Instantly, her boldness returned.

"Go on, go back to sleep, sleep it off," she said.

He threw aside the mottled blanket and came to his feet in a single motion. The woman made a show of recoiling from his nakedness.

"Lookit here, you!" she said. "I didn't come up here to—"

He went past her to the enameled sink hanging crookedly on the wall, sluiced his face with cold water, filled his mouth and spat, stared at himself in the discolored mirror. He picked up the smeared jelly glass from its clotted niche, but it shattered in his hand. He stared narrow-eyed at the cut on his palm, at the black-red droplets forming there.

He made a strange sound deep in his throat, whirled to look around the room as if he had never seen it before.

"Xix," he said. "Where are you?"

Wilma made a move for the door, recoiled as he approached her. He reached out, and with a precise motion, plucked the money from her hand. He peeled off a 10-dollar bill, thrust it at her.

"You'd better go," he said.

"Yeah," she said. Something in his voice frightened her. "Sure, I was just looking in . . ."

After she had gone, he stood in the near darkness, his head cocked as if listening to distant voices. He opened his cut hand, studied it. The wound was an almost invisible line. He brushed the congealed droplets away impatiently.

His clothes lay across the foot of the bed. He began to dress himself with swift, sure fingers.

6

In the prison dining hall, the guard Ted sat looking worriedly across the wide, softly lit room at the small corner table where, by long custom, Grayle dined alone. He had glanced that way a few moments after the lights had momentarily dimmed down, on an impulse to share the moment with the prisoner, grinning a satisfied grin that said, "See, we did it," but Grayle had been slumped back gripping the chair arms, his usually impassive features set in a tight-mouthed grimace. This had given way to a look of utter bafflement. Now Grayle sat rigid, looking fixedly at nothing.

Ted rose and hurried across. Close, he saw the sweat beaded on the prisoner's face.

"Mr. Grayle—you OK?"

Grayle moved his head slowly.

"You sick, Mr. Grayle?" Ted persisted. "Should I call the doc?"

Grayle nodded curtly. "Yes," he said in a ragged voice. "Get him."

Ted fumbled for the communicator clipped to his belt. Grayle put out a hand. "No," he said sharply. "Don't call. Go get him, Ted."

"Yeah, but—"

"Go and fetch him, Ted. Quieter that way," he added. "You understand."

"Uh, yeah, OK, Mr. Grayle." Ted hurried away.

Grayle waited for a full minute; then he rose, lifted the table, spilling dishes to the floor. With a bellow that rang in the peaceful room like a lion's roar, he hurled the table from him and, leaping after it, began overturning the unoccupied tables left and right.

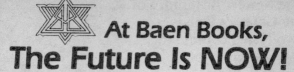